Out of this world

A delayed shock of realization ran through her as he raised his hand to his chest. He had only three fingers and a thumb. No room had been left for a pinkie. The long first finger tapped the boy's narrow chest. "Ahto."

"Cripes," said Paula. "Peter, he's an alien or something. He's not human."

Why couldn't this have happened yesterday? thought Paula. The most exciting thing of my life, and I've got to go to school! And what are we supposed to do with an alien?

Other Bullseye Books you will enjoy

The Believers by Rebecca C. Jones
Journey to Terezor by Frank Asch
Into the Dream by William Sleator
Letters to Lesley by Janice Marriott
A Tale of Time City by Diana Wynne Jones

Otto
from
OTHERWHERE

Peni R. Griffin

BULLSEYE BOOKS · ALFRED A. KNOPF
NEW YORK

Like everything,
this is for Damon

A BULLSEYE BOOK PUBLISHED BY ALFRED A. KNOPF, INC.
Copyright © 1990 by Peni R. Griffin
Cover art © 1992 by Doron Ben-Ami

Library of Congress Catalog Card Number: 89-38026
ISBN: 0-679-81571-6
RL: 5.7
First Bullseye Books edition: January 1992

Manufactured in the United States of America
10 9 8 7 6 5 4 3 2 1

Contents

CHAPTER 1

Midwinter Morning

Mist enclosed Ahto in a pocket of visibility just big enough to see the ground and an occasional sudden stone. Again he called the high, musical summons that should have brought the flock to him. The birdlike calls of the other boys, and the panicked bleats of the flock, were faint and directionless. He wished the mist would burn away a little so he could see where he was—no, he didn't. That would mean the sun was up and he had missed his ceremony.

A ewe appeared magically before him, her eyes ringed with white, and vanished before he could hold out his arms. He pursued her—uphill. The idiot beast was heading back to pasture, and she could run faster than he ever would, drat her!

This was all his own fault! All the boys had seen

the mountain cat at the same time, but only he had screamed. The head flockboy had shouted and thrown a stone, the cat had leaped back into the fog, and the flock—terrified by his frightened cry—had stampeded. His blood thudded noisily as he ran blind through the fog, but he could not outrun the shame.

Soon he had to slow his pace, confused. Was the bleating up ahead or more to his left? Ahto thought he heard flutes, the first bars of the Midwinter hymn that would sing the old sun to its rest and bring the new one in. Panting, he stopped. The lonely, magical sound should have been comforting, but he was lost, and he was late, and though they were singing the song—at least in part—for him, he could not even tell which direction it came from.

His grandmother said that the song opened rifts between the worlds through which strange creatures sometimes wandered. One had come through when she was a little girl, she said—an ugly dark girl-child, with five fingers on each hand and lumpy excrescences on her ears and nostrils. Grandmother spoke of this girl—Rose—kindly, but the thought of her gave Ahto a chill, of both revulsion and desire. One day, he would find the rift as it formed and walk through, exploring the lands on the other side, returning with new and lovely other-worldly tunes with which to honor the World Bird. One day, when he was grown up. The Midwinter hymn had more important meanings today. Till now he had never been allowed even to sing in public, but soon the red bird would be blazoned across his chest, and he would be a real priest—young, inexperienced, but a priest, nonetheless. The world would open up before him, and he would do great things.

What if—his heart paused a moment at the dreadful thought—what if he didn't get home till after the tattooing? One of the flockboys had had to wait two extra years for his ten-year tattoo, because the elders had decided he was too immature and irresponsible for it, and he had only been an ordinary boy. Priests had to be wise and reliable, and here he was, on the very day of his lifestaging, stampeding the flock and losing himself in the fog like a baby.

Ahto called into the fog again and kept walking. He couldn't think what else to do. Just a few weeks ago he had been so proud, so sure of himself! Everyone had been making grand predictions about his future. When his cousin Hahz fell and split his head open, Ahto stayed by him, remembering the right healing song and all the right notes, just from hearing his father sing it a few times. His father had said Hahz would probably have suffered serious injury, maybe died, if it weren't for Ahto. It wasn't just any priest's son who could have done that. How much would his helping Hahz weigh against this—and all the other silly things he had done in his life? Suddenly all his childish follies reared up, huge in his conscience, and he was certain that if he were late, he would be another year getting his tattoo.

Ahto began feeling his way downhill. He couldn't possibly recover the flock, anyway, as long as he was lost himself. If he could find his way into the valley and tell a grown-up what had happened, something might still be salvaged from this disastrous morning. The flutes and the singing faded in and out of his ears. The only other sound anywhere was the croaking of a raven. Despite his best resolve, his heart felt as cold as the bare parts of his skin. He thought about the warmth of the tattooing shed, and the feast at which the boys would be guests of honor. He had been supposed to get his flute that day, the instrument that would make him really a priest, able to talk to the World Bird. Maybe he should sing to the World Bird now, for protection and aid? It was a legitimate thing to do, but Ahto was reluctant to ask for help in getting out of a situation that was all his own fault.

The Midwinter hymn was barely audible. Ahto hesitated and tried a new direction, still downhill. Soon he could hear nothing but the croaking of the raven. He shivered inside the new festal garments his mother and sisters had worked so hard on—red poncho with a flight of white birds along the border; red leggings with a white stripe; soft, white loincloth and belted undertunic. They had expected to see him wear them at the ceremony today, expected to be proud. He called into the chaos of fog—for the head flockboy, for his cousin Hahz, for anyone!

The upper layers of fog were suffused with early sunlight, but Ahto couldn't see his own feet. He tried to hum to keep his spirits up, but the tunes he knew faded out against silence. Why couldn't he hear the Midwinter hymn? Had he wandered farther up than he had thought, gotten clear into wilderland? No—wilderland was steep and stony, and here he could hardly feel the ground below him.

When the surface leveled out, he stopped, bewildered. Surely he couldn't have gotten all the way into the valley? He called, and only that persistent, invisible raven answered. If he had been in the valley, he would have heard something, seen some tree or hogan bulking dark against the fog. This place was flat, as empty as the chaos lying between worlds.

He could only go on or stand still. If he went on, he was likely to walk in circles and get even more lost, while if he stood still—well, he was bound to be late now, one way or another. He had done his best and found himself wanting. Maybe the elders would let him advance his lifestage, after all? He felt bleak and dismal, certain that they wouldn't.

Ahto was just going to sit down and wallow in his misery a bit when he heard the raven again. The fog shifted to let him see something dark and straight thrusting upward off to his right. The raven groomed his wings atop it. Ahto had never seen anything that shape and size before, but strangeness was better than the void. He hastened toward it.

The shaft on which the raven perched was a tapering cylinder with a window tucked under a conical roof, but no door. If it was for birds, they had left none of the usual nesting signs. The big, black bird cocked an eye at him. "Good morning, Father Raven," said Ahto politely.

5

"Kark," said the bird. Many priests did not honor the raven much, because its cry was harsh and its eating habits unsavory, but Ahto's father had always asserted that all birds were sacred, the Death Croaker as much as the nightingale. Ahto rather liked ravens and was sure they had as much sense as people—something no one could say about most prettier birds. Besides, the stillness made him lonely and nervous, and he had no one else to talk to. He leaned against the cylinder—cold and rough on his skin—and said, confidingly: "I'm lost, Father Raven. Could you help me?"

The bird looked at him, pecked under his wing, and flew away, cawing regularly. Ahto followed the sound, hoping this was a providence of the World Bird's and the raven knew what to do with him. The fog shone now, shot through with light. Wet grass brushed his toes through his sandals, and the fog parted.

The raven hopped and pecked at a dark gray strip lying across the land. Beyond rose trees, some stark and gray, some in dull olive full leaf. It took him a while to put a name to the other features of the landscape. They must be hogans, he decided, because they certainly weren't rocks or plants; but they were not like any places to live in built by his people. They were in a variety of colors and materials, but were all made of combinations of rectangles, instead of the merry assortment of circles, squares, and triangles to which he was accustomed. Looking back the way he had come, Ahto saw the cylinder he had passed. Through the floating mist he could see that it rose straight out of a sheet of water, formerly hidden by the low-lying fog. A lake. He had walked up to and leaned against something in the middle of a lake.

Ahto stared at the cylinder. Maybe the fog had been as solid as it looked, and he had stood on it. What if he had stayed there another minute or two—long enough for the fog to thin as it was thinning now— would whatever force that upheld him have thinned also and dumped him into the lake?

Ahto began to shiver.

CHAPTER 2

The Boy in the Fog

Paula's alarm had gone off a quarter of an hour ago, but she was still curled tight under the covers, with her glasses on, staring out the window. Her room was in the front of the house, and most mornings she had a view across Woodlawn Lake to the YMCA. Today the universe ended a few feet from her window, vanishing in a roil of white fog.

This is the house on the edge of the world, she thought. We live on a cliff above the great white nothing, and we live on—on mushrooms that grow along the edge. We eat nothing but mushrooms, and our clothes are made of fog. In a little while I'll go to the spinning wheel on the hearth and make thread out of fog—

Nana stuck her head in through the doorway without knocking. She already had her makeup on, and her silvery perm was, as always, perfect. Anyone less like the grandmother of the girl who lived on the world's edge could hardly have been imagined. "Rise and shine, sleepyhead! Back to school today!"

"Just five more minutes?" begged Paula. "I'm still sleepy."

"The longer you stay in bed, Paula, the sleepier you'll be."

Paula dressed herself without enthusiasm. Fog meant cold, and cold meant jeans. Paula hated wearing jeans to school. She pulled her pink-and-cream sweater on and struggled with the lace collar that she had gotten for Christmas. At least from the waist up she would look like the person she was inside. Fully intending to release it later, she barretted her hair so Nana wouldn't start in about its getting in her eyes and needing to be cut. Across the hall Peter was throwing a fit about having to go to school.

Mama looked up from her newspaper and coffee long enough for her kiss when Paula came down. "Good morning, punkin. Ready to go back to school?"

"No," said Paula, "but I guess I'll go anyway." Two days after New Year's was too soon to end vacation. She helped herself to eggs and oatmeal off the stove. Ordinary oatmeal. "Could you make oatmeal out of mushrooms?"

"You could make a porridge, I guess," said Mama. "But it wouldn't be oatmeal. Not if you didn't put any oats in."

"Oh." She hadn't thought of that. Times like this

she was glad she had her own, ordinary mother instead of (as she sometimes wished) Mrs. Rimbaum. Amy's mother always dressed beautifully and laughed a lot, but one of the things she laughed at was stupid questions. When you came out with a stupid question, glasses and gray suits mattered less than a straight face.

Peter hurtled downstairs, cheerful again already. Nana followed sedately. "I get to ride my new bike today!"

"It's too foggy," said Paula. "We'll have to go in the car."

"I want to ride my bike to school!"

"Well, you can't, so shush."

"You can if the fog burns off some," said Nana. "Sit still and eat your breakfast, Petie."

Peter shoveled oatmeal down his throat. Carmen hopped into Paula's lap and shoved her head inquisitively into her plate. "Keep that cat off the table," said Nana warningly.

Paula shielded her egg from Carmen with one hand and ate with the other. She was trying to decide if she wanted to get a ride or go by bike. Biking through the fog would be romantic and mysterious—but less so, with Peter along, than if she were alone. Little brothers were deadly to mystery. If Nana drove them, they wouldn't have to leave till eight, and she would have time to read some of her library book. The children in it had been in the process of escaping from witch burners by opening an otherworldly gate when bedtime struck the night before. On the whole she thought she would rather do the extra reading.

Nana and Mama were discussing the exchange of one of Peter's Christmas presents, which was a nasty color and didn't fit. Suddenly Peter looked up and asked, around his oatmeal: "When're we getting our presents from Daddy?"

Paula wanted to hit him.

"Don't talk with your mouth full," said Mama. "How would you like it if I talked to you like this?" She loaded her tongue with oatmeal and said something incomprehensible.

Peter laughed, swallowed his mouthful, and pressed his question undeterred. "Will we get them today?"

"How should I know? I don't work in the post office."

"They probably got mixed up somewhere between here and Mexico," said Nana stiffly.

Paula didn't believe this and knew Nana didn't, either, and the last thing she wanted was to continue this discussion, so she said the first thing that came into her head. "I hope he doesn't send us a dog. Julie's aunt went to Mexico, and she found a stray dog there, a little bitty one that was real hungry and it followed her around. So she hid it in her trunk and brought it back to Houston and it got sick, and she took it to the vet, and he told her it wasn't a dog, it was a Mexican sewer rat. And she'd had it to sleep with her at night and everything."

"Ooh, gross!" exclaimed Peter happily. "Did she kiss it like Mrs. Stanley kisses her Chihuahua?"

"Now, I don't believe that for a minute," said Mama. "Julie's been telling you stories."

"But it's true! It happened to her Aunt Georgia—or maybe it was a friend of hers, but, anyway, it happened."

Mama was gathering up her purse and checking her makeup during this exchange: Now she stood up and walked around the table for good-bye kisses. "Have a good day, y'all. And you, buster"—she poked Peter in the stomach—"you be careful on that bike."

"Hurry up now," said Nana, glancing out the window. "The fog's clearing real nice. You don't want to be late your first day back to school, do you?"

Yes I do, thought Paula, but she knew better than to say it to Nana.

A distorting haze still hung over the morning when Paula and Peter took their bikes out of the garage, but passing cars were visible as beams of light and hulks of darkness at a normal distance. "You use your lights and be careful," warned Nana.

Peter shot out of the driveway and along the road that curved around the lake. Paula followed more slowly, keeping an eye out for them both. There were enough cars around at this hour that Peter only had to be an idiot in order to get himself killed—or run over that boy there, rising out of the haze on the lakeshore as Peter ran himself up on the grass. "Look out, you dummy!" she shouted, but it was too late. The strange boy cried out hollowly as her little brother plowed into him.

Paula pulled up next to them and watched as they disentangled themselves. "Y'all okay? Peter, you moron, why didn't you look where you were going?"

"I did look," declared Peter stoutly. "And I didn't hurt him. Oh, gross! He doesn't have a nose! Lookit!"

"Shut up!" hissed Paula. The kid, regarding them now with eyes as round and pale as the wedding-present china, certainly didn't need to be reminded of his deformities. He had no hair to speak of, only a fuzz of down thickening a little on top of his head. He had nostrils but no nose, just two holes flat in his face, and she realized with a shudder that his ears were the same way. He wore a red poncho and a scared, confused expression. Paula hastened to cover for her brother.

"Don't listen to Peter. He's just a stupid kid—"

"I am not!"

"Are you okay?"

The boy's lipless mouth moved, and sounds like birdcalls came out.

"See? He couldn't hear me," crowed Peter. "He just speaks Spanish."

"That's not Spanish," said Paula scornfully. "I don't know what it is, but I know Spanish when I hear it, all right." She eyed the boy warily, and he eyed her back. He looked unhurt, but skinny, cold, and scared. She couldn't just ride off and leave him.

A delayed shock of realization ran through her as he raised his hand to his chest. He had only three fingers and a thumb. No room had been left for a pinkie. The long first finger tapped the boy's narrow chest. "Ahto."

"Cripes," said Paula. "Peter, he's an alien or something. He's not human."

Peter's face lit up. "Maybe we can find his spaceship. You think we could go to school in a spaceship?"

"Ahto," repeated the boy, an anxious look in his pale eyes.

"What's he saying? What's an ahto?"

"Shut up a minute, can't you? I think it's his name." Hesitantly, Paula reached out her hand. The strange boy looked at it askance. "Ahto."

He smiled, making vigorous head motions. "Ta. Ta. Ahto."

Feeling like she was in a Tarzan movie, she pointed to him and repeated: "Ahto," then to herself and said, "Paula."

"Paula." The *p* was barely audible, due apparently to his lack of lip to pronounce it with. "Paula. Ahto."

"Don't forget me!" Peter bounced up and down on his bike, thumping his chest. "Peter, Peter!"

"Paula. Peter." Ahto pointed to each in turn. He had a tattoo—not a decal or an ink drawing, but a real tattoo—of a red feather on one palm and a red circle on the other.

Why couldn't this've happened yesterday? thought Paula. The most exciting thing of my life, and I've got to go to school! And what are we supposed to do with an alien?

"Come on, Peter," she said out loud. "We're going to be late."

"Who cares? I bet he'll show us his spaceship."

"How do you know he's got one? He may be from another dimension instead of another planet. And if we're late we'll get detention and won't have any time to go looking for spaceships this afternoon." Ahto was peering from one to the other with an air of concentration. Paula wondered if she appeared as anxious as that when Janie Santos and Nancy Reyes started giggling in Spanish. She got off her bike. Only one course of action occurred to her, and she didn't like it much. "We'd better take him to school with us. Come on, Ahto." She walked her bike a few steps, looked back, and beckoned. "Come on."

"Cuhn ahn." He followed uncertainly, staring constantly about him. Peter rode circles around them, his training wheels whizzing and catching on curbs. Paula wondered what Ms. Bingham would say when she saw Ahto. Would she turn him over to NASA or something? And what about the other kids? I suppose I could say he was my cousin Otto from somewhere and was born that way, she thought. Where do they wear ponchos? South America. That's no good. Somebody'd try to speak Spanish to him. Where is it down there they don't speak Spanish? Bolivia or Brazil? Brazil, I think. I think they speak Portuguese. He's my cousin Otto from Brazil. He didn't look at all Brazilian. Those eyes were kind of creepy, and the nose—gross! The boy met her eyes

15

and smiled anxiously. She smiled back, feeling guilty. "I sure wish you spoke English like all the aliens in books."

Ahto responded musically. Paula had never understood before what books meant by a musical voice, but he had one.

"Hey, Ahto!" shouted Peter, pedaling furiously. "Listen to this! Bell!" He rang the handlebar bell and shouted, "Bell! Bell! Bell!"

"Bell!" responded Ahto, mimicking Peter's shout and laughing. Paula patted her bicycle and said: "Bike. Ahto. Bike."

"Bahk."

"No. Bike. Watch my mouth. Bike."

"Bike."

"That's good. Um—" She took a fold of his garment between her fingers. "Poncho."

Ahto entered readily into the language lesson, and Paula became so interested that she forgot to hurry. The first bell rang just as they came in sight of the school.

"Oh, cripes! We're going to be late!" Paula started to run, pushing her bike ahead of her and banging her shins on the pedals. "Peter, you go on. And don't tell anybody we found an alien."

"You can't have him all to yourself!"

"I'm not trying to! He's too big to go in your class, so I'll have to take care of him. I'll say he's our cousin from Brazil."

"Nobody's going to believe he's from Brazil."

"Will you get on before you get detention?"

16

Paula's brother zoomed ahead as Ahto, visibly alarmed, hurried to keep up with her. She practically threw her bike into the rack and fumbled with her lock as the second bell rang. Ahto shifted from foot to foot, infected by her hurry. Grabbing her book bag with one hand and his arm with the other, she dragged him through the front doors, down the hall, and into Ms. Bingham's fifth-grade homeroom, bracing herself for silence and stares.

CHAPTER 3

Elementary Alien

For a moment, Paula thought that the sight of Ahto had created an instant riot; then an unfamiliar voice demanded silence, and she saw a stranger at the blackboard. A substitute! Relieved, Paula hustled Ahto to the empty desk behind her seat. He folded his narrow hands in front of him, looking around with an expression akin to shock.

Amy Rimbaum leaned across the aisle, staring at him. "What is that?"

"Who, not what," snapped Paula unthinkingly, and immediately repented. She was only on the fringes of Amy's group. If she offended her over Ahto, she lost an important base of support. "Be nice to him. He doesn't speak English."

"What happened to him?"

"Born that way," whispered Paula, as the room settled down enough for the substitute to speak.

"Good morning," she said, with more force than authority. "Ms. Bingham broke her leg skiing over Christmas, so I'll be taking her place for a week or two. My name is Ms. Tilley. I want each of you to stand up and tell me your name."

Everyone had noticed Ahto by now. Whispering and poking pervaded the room as the roll went around. Paula wished the empty desk had been beside her. For all she knew, on his planet sticking out your tongue was a friendly gesture. He could be offending the whole class this minute. Paula stood in her turn, said, "Paula Luther," abstractedly, and looked behind her as she sat down again. He stood up and said, "Ahto," with perfect aplomb. A look of revulsion passed quickly over Ms. Tilley's face.

"There's—ah—there's no Otto on this roll. Are you a new student?"

Ahto smiled fixedly under a barrage of stares and made a noise like a conversational grackle.

"He's my cousin," said Paula hastily. "Otto . . . Mayhew from Brazil." She shouldn't have used Nana's last name. Nana was active in the PTA, and lots of teachers knew a lot about her. Too late now. "He doesn't speak English yet."

"I don't have any record of him," said Ms. Tilley.

"Somebody must've forgot to write it down," blurted Paula. "With Christmas, and Ms. Bingham breaking her leg, and all."

Ms. Tilley looked at him doubtfully. "If he doesn't speak English, he'd be better off in a bilingual class."

"He doesn't speak Spanish, either. Just Portuguese." She wished she had remembered to take her barrettes out, so her hair could fall around her face and hide the burn in her cheeks.

"Did piranhas eat his nose or something?" called Dan Warner from the back of the room.

"I don't want to hear anybody picking on him about how he looks," said Ms. Tilley sharply. "Remember, he's a guest in this country. Who's next?"

The bell rang to leave homeroom and go to first period just as the roll call finished. Those who changed rooms shuffled out, replaced by people from other homerooms. The shock of the first sight of Ahto was visible on each face as it happened. Paula's stomach hurt.

"I don't get it," said Carla. "Why does he only have three fingers?"

"He's not really from Brazil, is he?" asked Roy Felder. "He looks more like a space alien or something."

"Where would Paula get a space alien?" scoffed Amy. Paula scuttled the idea of telling any of the children the truth.

"From space, dummy," said Renay Rios. Ahto's pale eyes traveled from face to face. Paula couldn't think of a thing to say to any of them.

No one seemed interested when Ms. Tilley introduced herself. "I'm sure you've all noticed that we have a new student," she added, as if she couldn't see everyone staring. Ahto watched Paula as the teacher explained about Brazil. "I'm sure you'll all want to be extra nice and help him find his way around." She paused, as if fumbling for words with which to confront his personal appearance, and proceeded with a helpless gesture. "Paula, why don't you share your book with him for now?"

Paula thought English class would never end. The disorder that always reigned under a substitute did allow her to teach Ahto a few more words. He seemed to be familiar with the use of books and pens, which was something. For all she knew, he might be from a planet where books were electronic, or a dimension where people wrote by making marks in wax with a stick.

At last the bell rang. Getting up to cross the hall for science class, they were instantly the center of a crowd.

"Hey, Otto!"

"Hey, you, Otto!"

"Where'd you get the tattoos, Otto? You a sailor or something?"

"Back off, y'all! You're going to scare him to death!" Paula felt his hand seizing her belt, as if he feared that the peering, insistent faces and hands would drag him away.

"Hey, Paula, you walk on one side of him, and I'll walk on the other, and we'll keep these creeps away," said Amy, taking over the situation with natural authority. For once it was a relief to get to Ms. Holubek's room. Nobody pointed or whispered in her classes.

Amy preempted Paula's explanation to Ms. Holubek. "He ought to be in special ed," the teacher said promptly.

"He's not retarded!" Paula exclaimed.

Ms. Holubek fixed her bright blue eyes on Paula, till she squirmed in her seat. "Special education is designed for children who can't keep up with the regular classes, and if he doesn't speak English, he can't, can he?"

"Hi," said Ahto suddenly. "Iz Holuvek, teacher."

The class looked at him, and he looked defiantly at the class. Someone in back giggled. Paula leaped at her opportunity. "You see? He knows lots of English already."

Ms. Holubek made a dubious noise and proceeded with the science lesson. Ahto seemed to follow the class better here, with its demonstrations and visual aids. Math, the next period, was harder—Paula spent large parts of it trying to explain which numbers were which to him, got called down for whispering, and knew no more about fractions at the end than she had at the beginning. It was a greater relief than usual when the bell rang for lunch.

Normally the group of girls that centered on Amy and her best friend, Janie Santos, ate in feminine isolation, but the addition of Ahto attracted more than attention. Dan paused at the end of the table to sneer. "You're going to eat with that? I'd throw up if I had to look at that face."

Amy put her nose in the air. Nancy Reyes looked

down hers. "We don't have wimpy stomachs like some people."

"Hey, at least I ain't a pansy like him."

"He is not!" Paula had no idea what a pansy was, other than a flower, but if Dan said it, it must be pretty bad. "You're a big, fat pansy yourself."

"I am not. Only pansies eat with girls." He stood over them like the shadow of death. Everyone believed Dan when he bragged that he would grow up to be star linebacker for the Dallas Cowboys, because he was already bigger than most sixth-graders. Everyone knew he didn't care what happened to him in the principal's office, and that the bruises he left lasted a week.

Ahto looked up at him, frowned slightly, and stood up between him and Paula. He didn't say anything, just stood. Next to Dan, he looked fragile, like a boy made of pipe cleaners.

Up to now Ahto had been something between a baby and a kitten, Paula's personal property. But of course he wasn't. He was a boy, and boys got into fights, and she couldn't move or help him because she was terrified of Dan and didn't know what to say. She didn't even know what Ahto understood of what was going on—whether he'd stood up to protect her from the class bully, or because he understood himself to be insulted, or for some obscure alien reason.

"Truth hurts, huh?" said Dan. "What you going to do about it?"

"He can't understand you, dummy," said Roy, putting his tray down next to Amy's. Kyle Buchman crowded into the seat next to Ahto, and Renay pulled a chair up to the end of the table.

Dan turned his dreaded attention onto the boys. "You going to sit with girls and that thing? Gross!"

"You're the only gross one around here," said Janie. Janie's brother was the biggest boy in the sixth grade, and she could say whatever she wanted to Dan. "If you don't like the view, you can go away."

Ms. Holubek popped out of nowhere. "Dan, find a place to sit and go there." She fixed him with her glittering eye, and he moved sulkily to a seat two tables away.

"Since when do y'all sit with girls?" asked Janie, leaning across Amy for the salt.

Roy poked a hole in his roll and poured sugar into it. "We're not sitting with you. We're sitting with Otto. Hey, Otto, you can sit down now."

Ahto was looking after Dan with an unreadable expression. Paula tugged at his long, belted shirt. He jumped and resumed his seat. Paula was pretty sure no one but herself noticed the sharp, appraising glance he cast around at everybody's hands before picking up his fork and tackling the pinto beans.

Normally sharing a table with so many boys would have been uncomfortable, but today everyone was quickly involved in teaching Otto to say "pinto beans," "fork," "roast," and so on. Afterward, on the playground, everyone was too busy running around keeping warm to do more than the most general shouting and pointing at him. If Kyle hesitated before grabbing that scant-fingered hand during crack-the-whip, Paula didn't notice; if Ahto jumped onto the merry-go-round at the wrong times during the game of color queen, no one held it against him; and he stepped into the center unhesitatingly during shake'em, performing as if he had played all his life. His voice rang out clear and sweet above the others, in rhythm, and almost properly pronounced. He spun with his eyes closed, poncho flapping absurdly, and staggered to a stop, pointing straight at Julie.

Ms. Holubek blew the whistle. Ahto jumped, clapping his hands over his earholes. "Line up now, line up!" she bellowed like a drill sergeant. She seemed to be annoyed at something. Paula wouldn't have thought anything of it, if the teacher's frown had not seemed to pass over her head to strike Ahto. She ran over his actions in her head quickly, but couldn't find anything that would have violated Ms. Holubek's code of conduct.

Today was a music day. Mr. Feinman, the music teacher, was entering the music room just as Paula and Ahto reached it, preceded by Renay and Kyle, followed by Amy and Janie.

"Good afternoon—excuse me—have a good Christmas?—hi, Paula, who's this?" He barely even looked startled, but accepted Paula's introduction calmly, for which she was grateful. "Brazil, hm?" he said, making a note in his roll book. "Just so he can follow the notes."

Ahto seemed to have grasped classroom procedure

by now, for he took his seat next to Paula, handled the music book with confidence, and spoke up with a creditable "Here!" when his name was called. When Mr. Feinman started talking—waving his arms around as he habitually did—Ahto watched the teacher's face intently, as if his eyes could interpret what his ears could not.

"I know how hard you all worked putting the Christmas pageant together," Mr. Feinman said, "and I just want to say that you did me proud. Now, to prove I'm not a slave driver, we'll take a day off and sing whatever you like."

" 'Down in the Valley'!" spoke up Amy at once.

" 'Bingo'!" exclaimed Roy, a split second too late.

"Ladies first," said Mr. Feinman, playing the first bar of "Down in the Valley."

Suddenly, Ahto's eyes lit up, and he sat straight on the edge of his chair, reminding Paula of a picture that her father had had of a dog pointing quail. As the class sang the first verse and chorus, Ahto was silent, except for a hum in the back of his throat. During the second verse he hummed louder, and the uneven chair he sat on rocked back and forth on its two longer legs, in time. He burst forth in the second chorus as if he could contain himself no longer, his voice rising clear and precise over the ragged sound around him.

"Know I lugh you, dear,
Know I lugh you.

Angels in heanen
Know I lugh you."

Every head swiveled, including Mr. Feinman's.
Somebody snickered, but Paula was too impressed by
Mr. Feinman's face to care. He looked as if he were
about to leap to his feet and cheer, but he swung into
the third verse and led off: "Build me a castle. . . ."

Ahto—startled by the reaction—fell silent, except
for that humming, until the third chorus, when he again
sang out clearly and perfectly:

"As he rides i, dear,
As he rides i.
That I nay see hin
As he rides i."

Mr. Feinman changed the tune to "Bingo," his
eyes fixed on Ahto's face. They seemed to share an
intensity of concentration, as if they could listen with
each pore. Hesitantly, but nearly flawlessly, Ahto joined
in on the first chorus. Even Paula could tell he was
matching the piano note for note.

She thought Mr. Feinman was going to say something when he finished that song, but all he did was
call for more requests and continue, giving preference
to repetitive tunes that gave Ahto a chance to listen
first and then join in. When the bell rang, Ahto was
grinning and rose to his feet slowly. "Paula," said Mr.
Feinman, "could you and your cousin wait a moment?

27

Don't worry about your next class. If I keep you late, I'll fix it."

Ahto waited expectantly. Paula's face went hot, for the children were looking back and whispering as they passed through the door. Amy's face was a curiosity beyond interpretation; she was not used to being left out of anything. Oblivious to the rest of the world, Ahto and Mr. Feinman faced each other with identical expressions on disparate faces. "Did your cousin ever take voice lessons?" asked the music teacher, not looking at her.

Ahto opened his mouth and let bird song out.

"I don't know," said Paula hurriedly, certain that whatever Portuguese sounded like, that was not it. "He sings real good, doesn't he?"

"He sings miraculously," declared Mr. Feinman. "Could you ask him—"

"I don't speak any Portuguese."

"Inconvenient. Otto—"

"Here?"

With one accord they sat down before the piano, Paula trailing irrelevantly behind them. "Now, I'll hit a note, and you sing after me. Do, re, mi, fa—sing, comprende?"

"Sing," warbled Ahto.

"Wonderful! Now." He struck a white key. Ahto's mouth opened like a lunar crater, his vibrating throat striking a sound that might as well have come from another piano. Mr. Feinman struck a black key; Ahto matched it. Mr. Feinman played scales, and Ahto followed him. Paula fidgeted from foot to foot, watching the hands creep around the clock face.

The clamor in the hall was dying down when Ms. Holubek led the principal, Mr. Bottoms, in. Paula's heart sprang into her mouth. As far as she was concerned, principals existed solely to discipline boys like Dan. If Ms. Holubek was going around giving Ahto a bad name, she'd . . . she'd . . . Cripes, what would she do?

"You'll see what I mean as soon as you see the boy," Ms. Holubek was saying. "Yes, here he is. Mr. Feinman—"

The music teacher looked up absently, his face alight. "Harvey, would you listen to this? Perfect pitch, that's what this boy has—perfect pitch, and incredible range!"

The principal looked at Ahto, who continued to match notes as Mr. Feinman continued to play. Paula wondered if her alien understood the look of disgust that passed so quickly over the principal's face. "We were just looking for this—um—child," he said. "Gina told me about him, and I was sure she was exaggerating, but I see I owe her an apology."

His face was heavy and sour, as if he smelled something bad. Ms. Holubek smiled a tight, nasty little smile.

CHAPTER 4

Invasion of the Grown-ups

The piano and the singer fell silent. Ahto gazed dubiously around at the clustering adults. Paula stepped up close beside him, feeling hollow.

"It wouldn't be easy to exaggerate about Otto," said Mr. Feinman enthusiastically. "I've never heard anything like him."

"I've never seen anything like him," said Ms. Holubek, looking at his face the same way she looked at messy math papers. "We'll have to send him to some other school, of course."

Ahto smiled anxiously at her, displaying his even white teeth. "Hello, Niz Holudek."

"What do you mean, some other school?" asked Mr. Feinman, just as Mr. Bottoms said, "I thought he didn't speak English."

"Don't seak English," said Ahto brightly.

"He's only parroting," said Ms. Holubek. "I wish your eyes were as good as your ears, Earl. Look at him. Of course he can't attend the same school as normal children. I don't know what Mrs. Luther could have been thinking about. She'll have to enroll him at Woodlawn Center."

"But he's not retarded!" burst out Paula, louder than she had intended. "I already told you he's not retarded!"

Ms. Holubek looked down at her out of blue and terrible eyes. "Shouldn't you be in class?"

"He's my cousin," said Paula defiantly, although her stomach felt wobbly and weak. She waited for somebody to tell her not to talk back and was surprised to hear Mr. Bottoms say, "I don't suppose it'll hurt her to miss a few minutes. Now—Paula—what can you tell us about this cousin of yours? Why didn't your mother come and discuss him with us?"

Paula could feel a tangled maze of half-truth closing around her. Desperately she clung as close to reality as she could. "I—I don't know. She's real busy, and we weren't expecting him. But he's real smart. He doesn't need to go to Woodlawn Center."

"A lot of people besides retarded ones go to Woodlawn Center."

"This is ridiculous," broke in Mr. Feinman, laying his hand on Ahto's shoulder. "This boy doesn't need therapy, just an English tutor and music lessons."

"He's disruptive," said Ms. Holubek. "Any child

that . . . unusual . . . is going to be. Not two hours ago he nearly got into a fight in the lunchroom."

"Dan picks on everybody," said Paula quickly. "You can't blame that on Ahto."

"She has you there, Gina," said Mr. Feinman. "If we're going to ship off disruptive students, I volunteer to drive that Warner boy over to the center right now. The world would be poorly served by sending natural talent like this one to a place where music is therapy. He doesn't need the stigma."

"He's going to have a stigma, wherever he goes," said Ms. Holubek crossly.

Mr. Bottoms glanced around from face to face, as if taking a vote. "Paula, what kind of school did he go to in Brazil, do you know?"

"Regular school," she answered stoutly. After all, he was probably perfectly normal wherever he came from, and if there were any school there, he would go to it.

"Well—the whole business is potentially complicated, and I wish Mrs. Luther had taken time to enroll him, but I don't see any reason to ostracize him for not having a nose. Got a piece of paper, Earl? Thanks. Now. Paula, I want you to give this to your mother the minute she gets home tonight." He composed a couple of scratchy lines, with much frowning and forehead wrinkling. "I'm sure everything'll be straightened out in a day or two."

Mr. Bottoms handed her the paper, folded into quarters, and she stuck it into her jeans pocket. Dismissed, she took Ahto off down the hall back to her homeroom, where study hall proceeded loudly.

The last two classes were without incident to distinguish them, but the last bell engulfed the pair in an eager, curious crowd. By the time they'd fought their way to the bike racks, Peter was already there, turning tight circles on his bike amid a mob of first- and second-graders. He skidded to a halt at the sight of them and cried shrilly: "See, I told you! We did too find an alien this morning!"

"Shut up, Peter!" shouted Paula. What was the use of telling lies all day with a little brother around?

"They wouldn't believe me!" Peter persisted, unheeding, as the crowd behind him surged forward.

"Leave us alone! Go away!"

"Don't seak English," said Ahto over and over, with an air of desperation.

"Ooh, gross!"

"Lookit his nose!"

"Little kids," sniffed Amy, but the authority of her scorn did not extend downward. Janie assisted to the extent of hauling her own little sister out of the tangle of faces and arms, dragging her bodily away; but the whole school was alerted and converging on the bike racks by now. Joe Santos loomed toward them, a few lesser big boys in his shadow, including Dan. Unprotected by Janie's influence, Paula was preparing to sell her life and honor dearly when unexpected assistance arrived in the form of Mr. Feinman and Peter's homeroom teacher, Ms. Ramirez.

"All right, all right, that's enough of that! Don't y'all have anything better to do? Scram! Scoot! Go home!"

"So this is Otto. Peter couldn't talk about anything but you all day. All right, you've seen him. Now go home!"

"Break it up! Break it up! Y'all want a lift home, Paula? We can put the bikes in the back of my wagon."

Nearly blind and deaf with rage, Paula accepted unthinkingly. By the time they departed the parking lot, Ahto in the front seat and Peter in back with her, she had calmed down just enough to isolate and attack the source of the trouble. "What'd you have to go telling the whole world about Ahto for?" she demanded.

Peter folded his arms and looked sulky. "Well, you took him off with you. You didn't share."

"You don't share people, Peter," said Mr. Feinman sternly. "Just because Otto doesn't have a nose doesn't mean he doesn't have feelings. How would you like to be mobbed wherever you went because people thought you came from outer space?"

"But he does!" said Peter. "We found him this morning and Paula wouldn't let me look for his spaceship and then she took him away."

"Peter, shut up!"

"There's no need to shout. You're scaring Otto."

He had indeed twisted around in his seat belt and was peering over the back with wide eyes and a perturbed expression. "Paula?"

"Sorry." Paula subsided against the door, heavily

uncomfortable. Mama and Nana would be home in a couple of hours, and what would she say to them—particularly with Peter in this mood? With sudden vividness she recalled their reaction when she had brought home the injured bat. What if they treated Ahto the same way—screams of outrage and out the door? The shock of this idea deafened her to all but the sneering tone of Peter's next remark, and she came in on the middle of Mr. Feinman's response.

"—to be telling lies."

"But I'm not," protested Peter. "She is. He's not our cousin. He's a space alien we found this morning. She told me to say he was our cousin, but I'm not going to tell fibs just for her."

What a time for him to go moral on her! Mr. Feinman was looking at Ahto rather more closely than he had previously.

"Mama'll be mad when she gets home. We should've looked for his spaceship," said Peter complacently.

They pulled up in the driveway. Paula unbuckled her seat belt. "Thanks for the ride, Mr. Feinman."

"No trouble." He cut the motor, adding, as Ahto struggled with his harness, "Your cousin doesn't seem very familiar with seat belts."

"They—uh—don't have them in Brazil." The sun was too hot on her sweater, and she was very tired. Mr. Feinman helped them unload the bikes. Ahto stood like a lost wraith, flat footed on the grass, staring around.

"Whereabouts in Brazil is he from?" asked Mr.

35

Feinman casually, setting Peter's bike on the cement and reaching for hers. "Bogotá?"

Paula, unable to remember the names of any Brazilian cities off the top of her head, took the path of least resistance and nodded. "Uh-huh."

"Bogotá's in Colombia," said Mr. Feinman.

"Oh," said Paula stupidly.

"Why don't you show Otto the house, Peter?" suggested Mr. Feinman. Paula gave her brother the key, and he dragged Ahto indoors. The alien looked back at the two of them, then shrugged and followed without fuss.

Mr. Feinman looked at Paula.

Paula looked at her feet.

Mrs. Rimbaum honked and Amy waved as they drove by.

"Let's make ourselves comfortable on the porch swing, and you can tell me all about it," said Mr. Feinman.

So Paula sat down beside him on the porch swing Granddaddy had built from a Handy Dan kit right before he died, and explained. She couldn't think of anything else to do. Mr. Feinman listened with a careful, neutral face, as if he were listening to an unfamiliar piece of music. He did not ask any questions until she'd finished, and then went straight to the heart of the problem.

"All right. What happens when your mother comes home?"

Paula scooted down in the swing. "I don't know."

"What do you want to happen?"

"I want Ahto to stay with us till he goes home."

"And you don't think your mother will let him?"

This was a hard way to put it. "We don't have any clothes to fit him."

"One way or another, he's a problem," said Mr. Feinman. "Much too big a problem for you to handle all by yourself, young lady, though I guess I can't fault you for trying." Paula felt small and incompetent. He smiled at her. "I'll call your mother at work and invite everybody to supper at my house, and we'll talk about it."

Supper started out to be a constrained meal, but Mr. Feinman moved cheerfully around his kitchen, making Mama and Nana sit at the table while he bossed the children, and it was hard to be uncomfortable around him. Ahto outdid himself, handling plates with care, practicing his English aloud. Nana could not take her eyes off him.

"What on earth made you say he was your cousin?" she asked. "And on my side of the family, yet!"

Paula had to puzzle over this awhile. "If Mr. Bottoms knew he was an alien, he'd give him to a lab or something." She surveyed the familiar grown-up faces, uncertain whether they would understand. Grown-ups could be thick at times.

"Yeah," said Peter, with ghoulish pleasure. "And they'd open him up and look at his guts and stuff. Like frogs."

"But, honey, what makes you think he's an alien?" asked Mama.

This degree of stupidity was more than she had expected. "Of course he is! He's only got three fingers and three toes and no ears or lips or—of course he's an alien."

"Some pretty remarkable people have been born in this world," said Mr. Feinman, tasting the spaghetti sauce. "That's why everybody believed you when you said he was born that way."

"People'll believe anything if you say it loud enough," said Paula, trying to sound like Nana.

The grown-ups laughed. "That's true, all right!" said Nana. "But, honey, what if he's not an alien? Someone must be looking for him. He may actually have been at Woodlawn Center."

"But he doesn't belong there," objected Paula, rummaging in her brain for a reason that would convince a grown-up. "If he did, he'd speak English. Look at everything he learned, just today. He couldn't do anything but those bird sounds when we found him."

"And nobody claims him?" said Mama to Mr. Feinman.

"I've been through the phone book. Police, hospitals, everything I could think of. The Health Science Center doesn't even recognize his syndrome. They're anxious to take a look at him."

"But somebody, somewhere, must be terribly worried."

"You'd think so. The problem is, who? And what do we do till we find that person?"

"I giff you glass off tea," said Ahto, naked brows wrinkled in concentration, as he set glasses down in front of Nana and Mama. Peter clattered the forks around and Paula assiduously stirred the spaghetti.

"Thank you, Otto," said Nana, enunciating clearly, as she did to small children.

"You're welcon, Nana." Ahto smiled.

Nana's eyes narrowed thoughtfully. "Paula, are you sure this boy couldn't speak English this morning?"

"Positive," Paula asserted. "All he could do was make birdcalls."

"Don't speak English," affirmed Ahto, spitting out the *p* with care.

"Then I don't think whoever had him deserved him," declared Nana. "He's sharp as a tack. Somebody needs to take care of him. Sally—I don't know why it shouldn't be us."

"Well—apart from the expense—"

"I could take him," offered Mr. Feinman eagerly, measuring oregano into the sauce. "Don't stir so hard, Paula. You'll slop hot water and scald yourself."

"But he ought to live with other kids," said Paula. "And we found him."

"Reckon my rainy-day money ought to get us well started," said Nana. "I don't grudge a little cash to help a child."

"Salad," said Ahto to himself. "Dressing. Ah, ah,

Bahcon Bits." Peter jostled him, and he almost landed in Mama's lap with the salad dressing. In rescuing himself from that disaster, he sent the salad bowl messily onto the floor and stood like one stunned, making a thin, piping noise like a grackle.

Peter burst out laughing at the sight of Ahto's horror-struck face, and the others followed despite themselves. Ahto looked around the kitchen, bewildered; then his thin mouth twitched, and a sound like water through a crowd of stones chuckled out. Nana started to collect the mess, but he politely forestalled her.

"Otto, you're a well-behaved little boy if ever I saw one," said Nana approvingly, watching him scoop up lettuce and cherry tomatoes.

"If you've seen any, it's more than I have," said Mama. "Peter, that was your fault. Give him a hand. You know, Earl, I don't see how we couldn't take him, under the circumstances."

"Hurray!" cried Paula, nearly jerking half-cooked spaghetti onto the floor in her enthusiasm. Ahto jumped at the sound, looked up at her glad face, and repeated, "Hurray?"

Nana laughed.

"I don't know what we're going to do about school, though," said Mama. "They won't take him without transcripts."

"You leave that to me," said Mr. Feinman, tasting the sauce.

CHAPTER **5**

Sweet Singing in the Choir

Ahto woke early—as he always did—and padded barefoot to the window. Peter was heavily asleep, his face mashed into the pillow and his legs tangled in the covers. Color was just now entering the room with dawn, turning the toys that littered the floor from gray to their natural brightness. Ahto closed the lid of the toy chest under the window and sat on it, looking out over the strange world he had landed in.

Six days had not accustomed him to the angles of the rooms or the stares of the people he met. For the most part he could not even interpret the faces that stared at him—peculiar, knobby things, which might be friendly, hostile, or indifferent, and himself none the wiser. Even Paula and Mr. Feinman were ugly and had no inkling of the most basic things. When he thought how Paula had expected him to eat bird—! If Renay had not taken it into his head to explain what a chicken was that day in the cafeteria, Ahto might actually have swallowed the stuff! That had been a long, confused, and dreadful day, so inexplicably horrible that he could no longer arrange its events in his mind. At least now everyone understood that he must not eat birds, though they all seemed to regard it as shamefully peculiar.

Ahto opened the window, letting in the chill morning air and the silence. Not quite silence—a raven sat in the bare limbs of a tree across the street, but his croak floated on the surface of the stillness, making no mark upon the depths of it. The only other birds in sight were the printed ducks rising endlessly across the curtains.

It's a good thing this happened to me, and not one of the other boys, Ahto thought, trying to call up the melancholy sense of his own importance that had maintained him so far. At least I know what reading is, even if I do have to learn brand-new letters. He had thought this so often that its comfort was stale. The other boys were properly tattooed and learning new skills at this moment, while he sat silent in a silent world.

The soft thump of Carmen landing in his lap startled him out of his preoccupation. Timidly, he stroked her head and back as Paula did, and the cat began to rumble, kneading his thighs as if he were a lump of dough. Her resemblance to the mountain cats disturbed him, but she was soft, and friendly, and too small to harm domestic flocks even if any were around—and none were.

"I think I know where I am," Ahto whispered to Carmen, hearing the cadences of his native tongue fall sweetly on the air. "This must be a village just for priests—and magicians. Father says there are no magicians, but there must be here, or we couldn't make those smelly metal wagons move without pulling, or hear music from a box, or bring cookfires out of air. That's why everyone learns to read and sing. Not very many people can sing properly, but I suppose most of those children are going to be magicians. The flocks and fields must be outside somewhere, and the farmers and herdsmen must bring tribute for all these priests and magicians to live on. I hear they do that in the river valleys. But who are they priests of, Carmen? It can't be the World Bird, or the rules would be the same. Is there a World Cat? Is that why you live with people?"

"Prr-rur-prp," said Carmen, arching into his hand.

The sky above the neighbor's hogan was stained with pink and blue. A boy on a bike tossed a bundle into the yellow yard below and rode on, pulling another bundle from the bag at his side. Ahto had seen him do the same thing yesterday. The bundle was called newspaper, and Nana complained about fetching it from the wet grass in her slippers. If he went and got it for her, she would be pleased with him. To please one's elders is always wise—and he liked Nana. Barefoot on the cold, wooden floor, he went downstairs. Carmen ran into Paula's room.

Nana was just coming down as he brought the paper in. "Good morning," said Ahto carefully. Then, remembering a phrase she had used each day when she found him up before the rest of the house, added, "The early bird gets the wurm!" He wasn't sure what he had said, but was gratified to hear her laugh.

"Good morning, Otto!" said Nana brightly, taking the dripping, plastic-covered paper from him. Her next sentence included the familiar term "breakfast," so he said slowly, "I am hungry." This appeared to be a satisfactory answer, and she allowed him to assist in her preparations. This was one strangeness that made sense to him. At home, he was not allowed inside the kitchen, because cooking was a skill belonging to women. Here, however, none of the things he thought of as male jobs—herding, butchering, hunting—seemed to be necessary, and if the housework were not split, there would be no reason to keep men around at all. He set the table and poured the orange juice, humming softly. The great rule was to be busy and not think about the world from which he was so inexplicably banished.

When the others started coming down, he wondered what would happen that day. The first four mornings had seen early risers, fully dressed, around the breakfast table, after which the day was full of going places to be stared at—school, people called doctors, big echoey buildings where Nana or Aunt Sally or Mr. Feinman had long arguments and strangers poked at him and set him pointless tasks. Yesterday, all but he and Nana had risen late and eaten in pajamas, and the day had largely been spent acquiring clothes in a huge, confusing storehouse. What happened on days when everybody came down early but in their pajamas, and the radio sang slow and stately music? He labored long over the question while eating his pancakes and finally decided he had formulated it correctly. He swallowed, turned to Paula, and asked: "What do we today?"

He caught four words of her reply: "We," "morning," "play," and "afternoon." "Play afternoon?" he asked.

Paula nodded vigorously. "And church in the morning."

Peter was shouting, but Ahto had learned to treat that as meaningless background noise. "Church morning?" he repeated, hoping for enlightenment.

Nana and Paula spoke across each other, garbling themselves so that the only word he caught was "singing." "Church singing?" he repeated hopefully, and felt his face grin all over when Aunt Sally (whom Paula called Mama) said, "Yes, lots of church singing."

Nana seemed amused at his enthusiasm, but Ahto didn't mind. Singing! No one around here seemed to take singing seriously enough—except Mr. Feinman, and Ahto was completely bewildered about when he could expect to see Mr. Feinman. One thing he knew: If he didn't want to be hopelessly behind when he found his way home, he must miss no opportunity to sing. If only—no, he mustn't even think about flutes. With considerable anticipation, Ahto finished his breakfast and followed Peter's instructions on donning the complicated outfit they told him to wear for church.

Church was a large white structure with a red roof.

Well-dressed strangers left their cars in the paved field behind it, walking as if something somewhere would break if they acted too natural. Mr. Feinman stood in front of a large, closed door talking animatedly to a bulky man with hair almost as sparse and pale as Ahto's. When he saw the Luthers he waved, calling. Nana marched Peter off to parts unknown, while Paula and Aunt Sally—looking remarkably alike, in pink dresses, square collars, and Nana-inflicted hairstyles—accompanied Ahto to the steps.

Ahto was too excited to hold his tongue or to mind the look the bulky man gave him. "Good morning, Mr. Feinan! Church singing today?" he demanded.

Not one word of the ensuing conversation could he follow, except that it was—like most conversations involving Mr. Feinman—enthusiastic and contentious. The bulky man, whose name seemed to be Verne (why did people have so many of those difficult lip-sounds in their names?), was nowhere near as hostile as Ms. Holubek, but he kept looking at Ahto and shaking his head.

Suddenly Paula, who had been standing by him, growing steadily redder and redder in the face, turned to him and said, in her fierce, defiant voice, "But Ahto wants to sing—don't you, Ahto? And you're a good singer."

Grasping gladly at this sentence, of which he understood almost every word, Ahto nodded and said, with deliberate precision, "I sing fery well. I can show you." He squared his shoulders and met the man eye to eye, as he would speak to an elder priest—after all, he could easily be an elder priest.

This appeared to be the right procedure, for Verne smiled suddenly, and he and Mr. Feinman took Ahto away from Paula and Aunt Sally, through bewilderingly unfamiliar halls to a room where a piano, racks of long, purplish robes, and coffee drinkers competed for space. The people there, of various ages, all turned their heads and viewed Ahto with identical shocked expressions. He held his head high and followed Mr. Feinman to the piano. The music teacher was talking, talking till the moment his fingers touched the keys. Ahto opened his mouth and repeated the bar he played precisely, even to the slight tinkle in the instrument, which his ear told him was probably a fault. He had been mimicking sounds, from the calls of birds to the clatter of pot lids, since the day he was born. Mr. Feinman seemed to think it quite an accomplishment, however, and he put in a little extra effort, to show what he could do. They ran through a few bars as warm-up, then Mr. Feinman spoke to the world in general, and began to play "Down in the Valley."

More people had begun to wander in. Ahto closed his eyes against their distraction, concentrating on pronouncing the meaningless words correctly. The tune was a simple one, and he had practiced it, as well as every other song he could lay mouth to, as often as he had quiet leisure to do so. When the song ended, he opened his eyes to a room full of stares. Feeling like a ewe in a ring of mountain cats, Ahto blinked around at them and smiled. His clothes were hot and heavy, and the back of his neck prickled with sweat.

Too many people talked at once, but the upshot was that Mr. Feinman steered him into a metal chair in a corner and sat next to him as the room settled into rows of people, holding open books the same color as the robes. Ahto frowned and racked his brains, trying to locate some purpose that could be served by his sitting in on the practice of priests so much older than he.

"Just like music class," Mr. Feinman whispered into his earhole and smiled encouragingly. Ahto looked back at him blankly, unable to make the sentence he thought he had understood fit reality. The old woman at the piano began to play, Verne began to wave his arms, and the rows of people began to sing.

"Be thou my vision, O Lord of my heart.
Naught be all else to me, save that thou art. . . ."

Ahto realized at once that, whoever these people were, they were not full priests. Where was the sonorous harmony—the intricate counterpoint—the—? Well, they were better than the music class, but they were not full priests! Verne might be. A motion of his hand cut off the music at the end of the verse, and another started it again after some talking and waving. Ahto watched and listened carefully as the verse was sung over. Yes—the arm waving definitely had some relation to the music, but not everyone seemed agreed about that relationship. Uneasily, Ahto realized that

Mr. Feinman had brought him here expecting him to sound better than most of the people in the room. Whatever reasons Mr. Feinman might have, Ahto did not want to disappoint him. He swallowed, sat up straight, and was ready with full lungs when Verne made them start over again.

"Be thou my bision, O Lord uff my heart.
Naught be all else to—"

Every eye in the room was fixed upon him again, and only he, Verne, and Mr. Feinman were singing. Ahto trailed off uncertainly, shrinking back into the corner. Had he screwed up the words that badly? Had he been meant to keep silence, after all? No; Mr. Feinman was speaking to the adults just as he had spoken to Dan two days ago, after that young annoyance had cornered him between classes and made him repeat strange noises on pain of arm-twisting. Verne appeared to support him. The woman played the first bars again; Mr. Feinman smiled; and no one turned around when Ahto ventured to sing his best.

They practiced four songs, a different sort of music from that sung at school, more like what he was used to at home. He was disappointed when Verne shut his book and everyone stood up. However, his curiosity was aroused when they started donning the purple robes over their clothes. "What do we next?" he asked Mr. Feinman, in an undertone.

The answer included the words "sing" and "church," but was otherwise unenlightening. Maybe they had to perform some ritual now before practicing any more? He allowed the piano woman to help him into a short robe and followed Mr. Feinman through more halls, humming his new tunes softly and smiling determinedly at all the people who stared at him.

The robed adults formed a double line in front of a broad doorway. Ahto, behind a barrier of purple backs, could see nothing beyond except a bright, arching ceiling. The church seemed to be full of meaningless, murmuring voices and elegant strangers. Ahto wished Nana or Paula had stayed with him. Mr. Feinman bent down and said something in his encouraging manner. The young lady beside him smiled as if it were her duty. The piano woman passed the end of the line, and soon great, rolling chords surged out from the doorway, completely unlike the sounds of any instrument Ahto could put a name to. The music filled his head with echoes of glory, the way music was supposed to. He strained forward to listen, whispering eagerly, "What is it?"

"That's the organ," said the young lady.

"Bach," said Mr. Feinman, his face bright. Ahto immediately divined that the young lady's answer was irrelevant and echoed the important word instead: "Bach!"

Pulled by the sound, the line moved into a room bigger than the village assembly hall at home. The piano woman sat at an instrument like two or three pianos mixed together, all keyboards, pipes, and slats. Ahto sat next to Mr. Feinman and peered around the man in front of him at a room full of rapidly filling wooden benches. The Luthers were just arranging themselves in the back. He waved, but only Peter responded, and he was immediately quelled by Nana. By leaning forward and twisting slightly, Ahto could see that he was in a sort of box next to an open space. A tall desk like the ones teachers used stood to one side, draped with a red cloth, an enormous book open on top. Urns of cool-smelling flowers decorated the space and two white candles waited unlit on a low, solid-sided table. On the wall hung a large wooden *T*—he recognized the shape from his efforts to learn the new alphabet. The same letter was stamped in gold on the songbook cover and decorated the cloth on the tall desk. It seemed a funny thing to display so prominently, the more so since Paula had told him that the capital versions of letters were more important, and this was shaped like a small *t*, with the crossbar going through the vertical line rather than resting on top. Maybe if he understood what church was about, he could figure out what it stood for. Under cover of Bach, Ahto stretched up to whisper in Mr. Feinman's ear, "What does *t* nean?"

"Shh," answered Mr. Feinman unhelpfully.

Two white-robed children bearing crook-shaped metal torches advanced up one aisle, lit the two candles, and departed down another aisle. A man in a black robe appeared unexpectedly next to the large *t* as the last chords of the Bach faded, and spoke in a clear, ringing voice. The crowd, which had finally stopped murmuring, responded in unison. The black-robed man folded his hands and bowed his head. Everyone in the room followed suit and sat quiet while he spoke gibberish in measured tones. Ahto stared at his own tidily clasped hands and tried to reconstruct in his head the last song they had practiced. They had hurried through it much too quickly. His back itched under his waistband. The grown-ups around him stood, and he jumped up eagerly, turning to head back to the practice room. Mr. Feinman caught his shoulder as the first bar of the first song they had learned filled the room. Backs straightened, lungs inflated, books opened, and Ahto realized with a shock that he was expected to sing in public.

For a moment, his mind was blank. Public singing before receipt of the ten-year tattoo was—well, it just couldn't be done. You might as well tell the sun to rise in the south. Did this place have no rules at all? He stared out between the purple backs in front of him, hearing only the roaring in his ears. A hand poked his shoulder. Looking up, he saw Mr. Feinman urging him to sing, his mouth forming meaningless words in his grotesque face.

"Thou my true father, and I thy true su uhn,
Thou inmie dwelin and I with thee one—"

Ahto could bear no more. He nipped under the side railing before Mr. Feinman could move and dashed out the doorway, heedless of the music faltering in his wake.

Through a hall blindly—into an open space bounded by double doors—someone following—through the door, tripping on his robe and nearly falling into a cool glare of sunlight.

CHAPTER 6

Father Raven

The world loomed huge and incomprehensible around him, nothing familiar meeting his eyes. Hearing his name called, he ran without trying to see, had a nasty moment when a car squealed angrily at him, saw live green, and ran for the color, shedding the robe as he went. Soon he sprinted up a straight dirt track between fences and cans of garbage, huge, toothy beasts clamoring on either hand.

The noise was intolerable. Ahto panted on, rousing a new batch of beasts every few yards. A glance over his shoulder revealed no pursuers, so he slowed his pace and turned at random as soon as he reached a paved road. Sore with running, he walked with his head down until he was alone with the cool silence.

Hogans, strange and at the same time monotonous,

surrounded him, endless squares and rectangles in square and rectangular plots of yellow grass. No one here knew how to live, or eat, or sing. The people were ugly and lumpy, with untidy masses of hair, too many fingers, too many nonsensical noises, too many eyes with which to stare at him as if he were the ugly one. He slapped his hard, stiff new shoes against the pavement, making an angry noise that the winter silence swallowed. Above him, the sky soared blue, high, and bare. Around him, the world was full of angles and dull trees.

A child on a wheeled board trundled down the strip of pavement laid through the grass, looked him full in the face, cried out shrilly, and backrolled as fast as his foot could move. "Nobody asked your opinion," said Ahto crossly, in his own language. The whir of the wheels died away in the distance, but the high-pitched yells continued. Ahto turned on the next crossroad, head down, hands in his pockets.

How long or far he wandered before he found the open space, he could not tell, but he was tired and beginning to be hungry. The outline of a hogan was marked in the rank yellow and green grass, a smooth gray tree rearing up where the front hall would have been. Ahto climbed the three broad steps that were all of the structure remaining and dropped off the back to sit, hidden from the street, with his knees drawn up and his head down.

A raven croaked nearby, but he didn't look up. His eyes and throat prickled. "I want to go home," he said to his knees. "I want to go home right now."

"Wanting's not much use in this world," said a harsh voice—not unkindly, but as if burdened with laryngitis.

Ahto jumped and looked around. He was alone except for the raven, who stood with his head cocked and his neck feathers ruffled. "Good morning, Father Raven," he said perfunctorily.

"You don't look like you think so," said the bird, "but I'm glad to see you remember your manners."

Ahto opened his mouth and closed it again.

"Prrk," said the raven, as if laughing. "Don't stare, boy! It's rude."

"I'm sorry, Father Raven." Ahto blinked rapidly. "How can I understand you? I haven't been granted the speech of birds—have I?"

"You're right about that! No, all riftfarers can speak to each other, whatever shape their mouths are."

Riftfarers. Ahto leaned forward. "Are you the raven I saw in the fog on Midwinter Day?"

"Got it in one." The raven hopped closer. "I don't like to mind other folks' business, but I just thought I'd keep an eye on you, for old sake's sake. You were always good about leaving out a share to feed the ravens along with the pretty birds—and it's not everyone thinks of us, not even among priests." Picking under his wing, the bird made another laughing sound. "So you see, it's true what they say about good deeds returning on you."

"Do you know how to get home?"

"Yes," said the raven coolly, "for all the good it'll do you."

His uprush of happiness thus abruptly checked, Ahto so far forgot himself as to demand, rather than ask: "What do you mean?"

"I mean," said the raven, looking down his beak at the boy, "that you can't just walk the rift whenever you feel like it. Maybe you and I together could find it if we looked, but where we'd wind up if we went through is another matter. Not your home, wherever we went."

Ahto sank back. "Then—I can't go home?"

"Not just whenever you please, you can't." The huge bird seemed unable to keep still. He hopped, and preened, and fidgeted all the time he spoke. "It'll open up for you sooner or later, following its own rules, if you just catch it at the right time."

"What rules? How can I tell the right time?"

"It'll not likely happen till Midwinter. What you need is a song at one end and a fog at both. The rift can't open without a fog."

"Why?"

The raven jerked his tail. "Who do you think I am, the World Bird? Why should rain fall down instead of up, or the sky be blue instead of pink, or these people have hair and me feathers and you some sort of down that can't be called either? I just follow the rules. I don't make them."

"I'm sorry, Father Raven."

"S'all right. No harm in wondering, but it's no

good asking me. All I know is, if there's a fog at both ends when the Midwinter hymn—or something equally strong—is sung, you can walk through; but if not, you can't. But you see you've got a wait ahead of you, and it's no good throwing fits and wishing."

The prospect was indeed daunting, but Ahto wanted to show this bird that he could be brave and sensible. "I guess I can manage for a year," he said uncertainly.

Father Raven looked him up and down with one bright eye, then turned his head and looked him down and up with the other. "It might be longer than that. There might not be a fog here at the right time."

"There's always fog at Midwinter."

"These people have a saying: You don't like the weather, wait awhile. You can't tell what the weather'll do from day to day around here, much less year to year."

"Oh," said Ahto.

Father Raven hopped, flapped, and landed on his knee. Ahto gulped and held absolutely still. "Always best to face facts," said the bird. "You have to live with them, one way or another. This isn't such a bad place, once you get used to it."

"I don't think I'll ever get used to it." Ahto sighed.

"What was all that about this morning? You nearly got killed, running out into the street like that. What'd they do to you that was so horrible?"

"They wanted me to sing in public."

"Don't you like to sing?"

"I don't have my ten-year tattoo."

"I see. But nobody has tattoos here, you know." The raven's feet were sharp through the fabric over his knee. "Let me tell you about music on this side. Not one person in a hundred hears or understands music as well as a three-year-old priest on your side, but anybody can try to make it, anywhere. They'd as soon think of restricting your right to breathe. Nobody'd think twice if you sang in public."

"I would," said Ahto. "Maybe these people are different, but I'm not. If it's not right for me at home, it's not right for me here."

"You'll never make them understand that."

"I know."

"So what are you going to do, now you've run away?"

"I don't know."

"Those folks you live with are going to wonder what happened."

Ahto's stomach wiggled with shame. "I must've embarrassed them to death."

"I reckon they'll be more worried than embarrassed. They like you, you know."

"Nobody else does!" Suddenly the remembered heat of those curious stares burned his skin more than the reality had.

"People who don't like you don't matter," said the raven glibly. "If you're going to insist on being depressed, you can do it alone. That girl who went from here to your valley didn't have life any easier than you, but she got through it all right. I don't see why you can't."

Ahto had almost forgotten this legendary personage. "Did you know her?" he asked, suddenly hopeful. "Where is she?"

Father Raven hopped back to the ground. "Somewhere around. I can't keep track of people. She'd be an old woman by now."

"But she does live here? And she can talk like a real person?"

"She could speak your language when she left, all right. She's either still in town or moved somewhere. It's no business of mine. How can you sit so long without eating? I'm about to starve to death."

Ahto's stomach growled. "If I have to live here for a year, I guess I'd better stay with the people I know. Do you know which direction church is in?"

"Reckon if you head that way somebody'll find you." Father Raven jabbed at the air with his beak. "I've got to go find something to eat."

"Thank you, Father Raven," said Ahto humbly, rising. "It's good to talk to someone I can understand, for once."

"Prrk!" Father Raven flew into the lower branches of the naked tree. "I understand you, young man, but I doubt very much if you can understand me!" With that he clapped his broad, shining wings and launched into the sky.

Ahto watched him flap and soar away. He was still not happy, but his unhappiness was quiet and supportable. He started off in the direction the bird had indicated.

He was certain he had walked much farther than he had coming out to begin with, when, tired and hungry, he heard a familiar voice calling the local version of his name. "Otto! Otto! Honey, where are you?"

"Nana!" he called back, and they found each other in a few minutes. The old woman ran up to him, her usually tidy hair straggling around her face, and amazed Ahto by clasping him close, as if she were his grandmother. A torrent of incomprehensible words in a comprehensible tone deluged his ears. Father Raven had been right—they had worried about him! He dug in his brain for the proper words of apology, hugged her back, and said: "I'n sorry, Nana."

She looked at him, her oddly shaped brown eyes all fluttery and wet around the edges, then abruptly took his hand in her broad, soft one and hurried him along, still talking.

Whatever things went on in church seemed to be over, for people were drifting around outside now. Peter and Paula stood on the steps in front of the double doors with the black-robed man. When they heard Nana's triumphant call, they left him there and ran to meet them, Paula shouting almost as loudly as Peter. As they dragged him into a suddenly coalescing crowd, Ahto had the uncomfortable realization that they must have had the whole assembly involved in looking for him. Feathers, why hadn't he just sat still and refused inconspicuously to sing? He clung tight to Nana and shut his eyes against the unreadable, enclosing faces.

"Leave him alone," said Paula, bulwarking him from the other side. The black-robed man led them into a room full of inexplicable objects and shut the door against the inquisitive world. He produced grape juice from somewhere and proceeded to hand it around. This man must be someone important, to have stood up and directed the ritual, Ahto thought; he should probably be honored. Unable to summon the proper feeling out of his tattered nerves, he resorted to politeness. "Thank you," he said, carefully composed a full sentence, and added: "Where is Mr. Feinman and Aunt Sally?"

"Looking for you," said Paula.

Nana and the robed man talked overhead while Peter fidgeted around the room and Paula and Ahto sat on the edges of their chairs, drinking grape juice. "Are all ticked at me?" Ahto asked, in an undertone.

"No, but you were a dummy to run away." Ahto knew "dummy" was not a nice word; but she didn't sound angry. He smiled at her tentatively and tried to make a sentence that would explain.

He was still trying when Aunt Sally burst through the door, Mr. Feinman close on her heels. Ahto didn't even have a chance to open his mouth before they pounced on him, searching for injuries and babbling. Mr. Feinman seemed to think he owed Ahto an apology, rather than the other way around, and repeated the phrase "stage fright" over and over. Eventually Ahto got someone to define this and tried to explain that it wasn't true, but his stock of words proved inadequate to the task, so he gave up and remarked that he was hungry.

This soon led to a return to the car, but the day's bewilderments were not over. Instead of going home, they followed Mr. Feinman's car through a confusion of streets to a cafeteria, infinitely superior to the one at school. Women in bright clothes gave Ahto everything he pointed to from an array of mysterious food, and Mr. Feinman found them a corner out of the way of the other diners, where few could see him to stare.

An idea occurred to Ahto as he sat, alternating between sopaipillas and tamales. Anyone in the room who saw him, sitting at a table with a cluster of people about him, would assume that he was in the midst of his family. The hypothetical stranger would think that Mr. Feinman and Aunt Sally were married, and that Ahto was their son—brother to Peter and Paula, grandson to Nana. Ahto would be a normal, if unusual, part of this world. He pretended that it was true, smiling around at his family possessively.

"You look happy." Aunt Sally smiled back. "What're you thinking about?"

He couldn't possibly have expressed himself, so he fell back on another thought. "I saw a bird," he said, enunciating carefully. "A big, black bird."

"A grackle?" said Paula.

Ahto shook his head. Grackles were common, smaller than Father Raven and different in many small ways. "This big," he said, holding his hands nearly two feet apart and imitating the bird's laugh. "Prrk! Prrk!"

63

"A raven," said Nana promptly. "I saw one yesterday," and her sentence turned into gibberish.

So Nana had seen him, too. Ahto poked a hole in another sopaipilla and poured honey into it, resolved to take advice and face facts.

CHAPTER 7

Bad Morning All Around

In the next few weeks, Ahto faced more facts than he had ever known existed. His spoken English improved by leaps and bounds, driven by necessity and assisted by a trained ear. Numbers were a problem until he grasped the difference between counting from a basis of eight fingers and counting from a basis of ten. Aunt Sally commended him mightily and showed him how any number could be taken as a base. This accomplishment gave him confidence for a whole week.

English class finally settled down when Ms. Bingham took over from Ms. Tilley. She was patient and kind, and did not once mention putting him in a slower class where he wouldn't have Paula to help him. At home, he had read quite well; here, he could only watch helplessly as Paula's eyes traveled quickly and efficiently over a page, absorbing everything on it like a sponge. Even Peter read better than he did.

"Never mind," said Kyle encouragingly, when he complained about it at school one day. "Dan's known English all his life, and you read as well as he does."

Ahto recognized this as a joke from Kyle's tone, and smiled politely, but mention of Dan was not calculated to cheer him.

For the most part, the world could be divided into armed camps. His friends at school clustered around him and made an only partly effective barrier against the Dan Warners of the world—the starers, pointers, and shouters. "Just ignore them," Nana told him repeatedly, without giving any instructions on how to ignore balls aimed forcefully at one's stomach, or feet maneuvering to trip him in the aisle. Some people couldn't be put into camps, like Amy and Janie, who on the one hand defended him and on the other laughed at his *m*'s. Some days he came in from recess trembling all over.

Alone out of all humanity, it seemed, Mr. Feinman had some conception of proper priorities. Ahto visited him on weekends, dropping by for an hour or two at a time, and Mr. Feinman not only helped him practice but fed him that for which he hungered. Music was readily available, but that which came out of the radio was for the most part too alien to hear properly. Ahto couldn't even tell which pieces were supposed to be good. Mr. Feinman, however, had albums and a stereo, which in magical combination produced sounds Ahto could admire, if not altogether comprehend. Bach—Mozart—Haydn—he became casually familiar and enthusiastic about names that made other children—even Paula—look blank or laugh derisively.

What with this good thing, and that bad one, Ahto learned to cope; till one Saturday morning life began to go wrong.

This was partly his own fault. He had begun to understand the concept of television—a bizarre, hypnotic bit of magic that made his eyes ache. The night before, he had been drawn into a movie Aunt Sally had turned on, sucked in by music he recognized. The story was about Mozart, who had made the music, and the evil musician (a profoundly disturbing idea Ahto took half the movie to grasp) who wished, from jealousy, to destroy him. At bedtime he had been on unbearable hooks of suspense and begged so hard to finish the movie that Aunt Sally let him, with the result that he had gone to bed late, spent a night haunted by evil musicians, and rose with a headache after the sun was already up.

When he got out of bed, he stepped onto a toy truck Peter had left out. "Ow!" he shouted, and glared with unregarded ferocity at the lump under the spread that was all Peter amounted to at this hour. He dragged one of Nana's phrases out and threw it across the room. "I wish you'd learn to bick ub your things."

Peter grunted, revealed a single bleary eye, and made an indistinct smacking sound. Ahto, who had braced himself for a screaming match, was discon-

67

certed, but not yet so cranky as to push the point. Instead he dressed noisily and thumped downstairs. Piles of waffles waited on the table. Aunt Sally was just hanging up the phone. "There you are, Otto! That was Mr. Feinman. He wanted to make sure you knew not to come over today. He has to run up to San Marcos."

Ahto, who had counted on Mr. Feinman to explain the evil musician to him, felt affronted. This was the first time the music teacher had ever run off and made himself unavailable. He spilled syrup on his place mat as he asked: "What's Sannarcos?"

"Oh, Lord! Here, wipe it up, quick! It's a town not far away. A friend of his had an accident last night, and Mr. Feinman's gone to visit him."

"Oh," said Ahto.

"He might drop by this evening, and he'll be at church tomorrow. You can spend one day with kids your own age, can't you?" Aunt Sally was in one of her bustling moods and didn't wait for an answer. Instead she looked at the clock. "Shoot, it's getting late! And I've got so many places I have to go today!"

Nana appeared, fully dressed, hair drooping. "I can't find my curling iron, Sally," she said, kissing them both good morning. "You didn't borrow it, did you?"

"I gave up on curling irons years ago, Mama—you know that." Aunt Sally brushed a straight lock out of her eyes and took a big bite of sausage and waffle. The washing machine thumped and whirred in the background.

"If I don't find that thing soon I'll have to go to

work like this," said Nana, cutting up a waffle and spreading the pieces with apple butter. "The hair of beauty parlor owners shouldn't flop."

"I'm sure your reputation will survive one day of drooping perm," said Aunt Sally.

"I think Paula has it," said Ahto, suddenly remembering.

"Paula?" Nana looked surprised. "She knows she's not allowed to use that."

Ahto was certain he knew what they were talking about now. "She and Amy were going to make her ringlets like sone girl in a book last night, but they bracticed on a Barbie and it didn't work."

"I bet it didn't!" Nana looked stern. "I think it's about time that girl got up." She pushed her chair back forcefully, leaving her breakfast half eaten.

Paula came down about the time Ahto was rinsing his plate, while Aunt Sally unloaded the washer. "Good morning," he said.

"Don't talk to me, you tattletale!" snapped Paula, throwing waffles at her plate.

Ahto blinked. "What's a tattletale?"

"You are! What'd you go telling Nana about the curling iron for? It wasn't any of your business."

Ahto had seen Paula angry many times, but that had always been anger for, not at, him. He stood, stunned. "She asked," he said. "She wanted to find it."

"You didn't have to tell her and get me in trouble!"

"Paula, don't shout at Otto," said Aunt Sally, carrying in a basket of wet clothes. "It's not his fault you

69

did what you weren't supposed to. Otto, would you do me a favor and hang up these clothes? I've got so much to do I don't know where to start."

Ahto left Paula chewing a waffle and staring sullenly at the ceramic ducks over the stove. The air in the backyard was not warm, but the sun shone clear and yellow. Paula wasn't being fair. He hadn't known telling Nana would get her into trouble. You had to answer when grown-ups asked questions. He wished Mr. Feinman were going to be home. How long was Paula going to be mad at him? How was he going to get through the day without either of them? The grackles argued in the alley as he hung Peter's T-shirts in a steaming row. He had never in his life hung clothes to dry before he came here. It was girl work. Funny how he hadn't minded doing girl work for these people before. At home he would have been in the smelly, fluttery warmth of the aviary by now, doing proper priest work, not menial chores.

Ahto finished quickly and went in, to find Peter complaining loudly because Carmen had dragged the remaining waffles onto the floor before he'd had any; Aunt Sally telling him that they were stone cold anyway and he should have come down earlier; and Paula telling him not to be a crybaby.

Nana left for work. Peter ate cereal, grumbling. Paula tried to talk Aunt Sally into taking her along on the errands and leaving Ahto in charge of Peter. Ahto went into the living room and fiddled with the stereo, trying to find a station that played music he understood. Outside the sun had gone behind a cloud, and the lake lay across the horizon like a sheet of lead. A funny-looking car, shaped like a bug, with a passenger door that was a different shade of red from the rest, drove slowly around the curving street. A group of big boys, carrying mysterious things, straggled by on their way to the YMCA. The radio spurted Spanish, a newscast, and a commercial for an airline. Aunt Sally poked her head into the living room. "Otto, I'm going now." The red car pulled up in the driveway behind Aunt Sally's car.

"Who's that?" asked Ahto.

She looked where he pointed, and a peculiar change came over her face, as if were slowly freezing. A tall man, in a T-shirt and grubby jeans, with his arms full of packages, started across the grass. "It's Tom," she said blankly.

"Who?" asked Ahto; but Aunt Sally was gone. He heard her calling through the halls; heard Paula and Peter shouting; saw them bursting out the door, shouting: "Daddy! Daddy!"

Ahto had never heard the word before. Watching from the window, he thought he saw a resemblance between this man and the picture Paula and Peter kept in their bedrooms. The mystery of his identity had been overlooked, in the midst of so many other, more immediate ones. He stood in the living-room doorway as the others dragged the stranger into the front hall. He seemed cheerful and friendly enough; greeted Aunt

Sally jovially, and passed out packages. The children tore into theirs, but Aunt Sally laid hers on the hall table without glancing at it.

"Better late than never, I suppose. I've got to get a move on, Tom. Lots to do."

Tom spoke torrentially, too quickly for Ahto to catch much, oblivious to Aunt Sally's suddenly increased hurry. "Bye, then," she said, breaking forcibly across the stream of words. "Paula, don't forget to lock up. Have a good day at the zoo." She dived out the door, then backed up and said, crossly: "Tom, get your car out of the driveway."

Instead he talked more, waving his arms and smiling. Aunt Sally frowned, walked stiff backed to her car, and made scars in the grass driving around his.

Ahto stood still while Peter shouted over the candy and brightly painted, noisy gourds that came out of his package, and Paula collected jackets and her purse. They were going somewhere. Was he invited? He couldn't understand one word in ten Tom addressed to the others. The man had not noticed him, and Paula was still sullenly avoiding his eyes. Who was this person? Should he stay out of the way or attract attention? Tom's eye fell on him during the struggle to insert Peter into his jacket.

His eyes were dark brown, like Paula's. At the sight of him they flew wide open, and the face around them jumped in surprise. "What is that?" he asked quite clearly, and then, less comprehensibly, "The Creature from the Black Lagoon?"

"It's Ahto, Daddy, that's Ahto," said Peter, jibbing unhelpfully with his sleeves half on.

Paula granted him one glance, set her mouth stubbornly, and said: "He's a tattletale," before exiting as precipitately as her mother. The screen door slammed behind her.

Ahto's skin grew hot with embarrassment. The man made none of the usual grown-up attempts to subdue his expression. Stepping forward, Ahto held out his hand politely and said, carefully: "I am Otto. I am—"

Tom appeared not to notice the proffered hand and interrupted genially. "I'm Mr. Luther, Peter and Paula's father. Nice to meet you, but you'd better go home now. I'm taking them to the zoo."

"I am," said Ahto, but Peter's attempted shouts of explanation drowned his words and confused his thoughts. Mr. Luther raised his voice easily over the ruckus.

"Doesn't Ahto get to go, too? Why doesn't Ahto get to go, too?"

"I can't take the whole neighborhood, Peter. Besides, he'd scare the animals. Come on, both of you. Out we go. Don't just stand there with your mouth open. I don't want to look at your tonsils. You'll have to go home now, Otto."

In a daze, Ahto followed the wake of his words. Paula sat in the backseat of the car, arms folded and head tilted back to stare at the ceiling. Ahto stood on the porch as Mr. Luther hustled the protesting Peter into the front seat, talking constantly, and drove off.

73

Ahto looked after the disappearing car. The sky was gray, the world around him silent, the breeze off the lake chill. Paula had not stood by him.

He wondered if there were any way to get over being a tattletale.

Carmen chased the neighbor's Chihuahua across the yard, the dog's shrill yap skipping over the surface of the silence. Ahto felt naked, standing in the middle of this huge, flat world. How many eyes stared at him from behind those rectangular windows? Paula had not locked the door as she went out. Ahto went inside.

He had never been alone in any building anywhere before. The stereo was making a sound that clashed against his eardrum—a twangy, unfamiliar instrument and a nasal voice droning about cheating. Ahto turned the noise off and wandered around the house. He had homework, but without Paula to help he didn't care to approach it. If she never forgave him, she'd never help him again. The washing machine stopped. I ought to go hang those clothes up, he thought.

Suddenly Ahto just wanted to go away, leave, be someplace else, no matter where. Someplace he had never been before, someplace where no one and nothing stood between him and the cruel secrets of this world. You couldn't rely on other people to shield you. Not even Father Raven. He hadn't seen Father Raven since the day he ran away from church. Other people had other interests to tend to. Well, he could go off and leave people, too!

Fetching his windbreaker out of the hall closet,

Ahto distributed his money among his pockets. Aunt Sally gave him the same allowance she gave Paula and had explained to him about money. He knew each piece, and how many of the other pieces it was worth, and even understood about buying, though he hadn't made any purchase larger than a candy bar. He had accumulated five dollars and seventy cents, mostly in change, and had no idea whether or not it was a lot with which to face the world. Well, he'd just have to find out! Resolutely, he walked out the front door, making sure he pushed the lock button, and pulled it fast shut behind him.

CHAPTER **8**

Solitary Saturday

Ahto walked around the lake, across the creek, and under the broad stone arch over the road by the YMCA. He considered following the creek, then saw a metal flag a block or two farther on. Paula had told him that these flags indicated bus stops and pointed out a bus to him—a huge car that roared and groaned around the city, giving people rides. He should be able to get far away on a bus. He sat down on the sidewalk, under the metal flag, and waited.

The buildings on this side of the arch were businesses, places people didn't go to on Saturdays if they could avoid it, and with the exception of the occasional passing car, he was alone. He ran his voice up and down the scales a few times, then practiced his local songs, then sang "The Battle of Narrow Pass" straight through from beginning to end. This ballad was very long and mentioned his great-grandfather by name.

An amazing number of cars looked like buses in the far distance. A bus went by on the opposite side of the street, come and gone before he could run across to it. He had almost decided to walk after all when a real bus loomed on the horizon. He stood, filling his fist with change.

The doors hissed opened. Ahto climbed the steps and asked the woman behind the wheel: "How many cents?"

"Forty," she said, her eyes flicking quickly over him and settling on a spot above his head. As he dropped the proper change into the glass box and turned down the aisle, a little boy screamed. His mother slapped him and loosed a staccato torrent of Spanish. Ahto sat down quickly and looked out the broad window, pretending he didn't care. The bus lurched and continued down the street.

An old woman with a straw purse smiled at him. "Don't you pay that kid any mind," she said. "It's no good letting them rile you. My boy was born with a harelip, and he gets that sort of thing to this day, but he just doesn't let it rile him."

Ahto understood the main thrust of this speech to be friendly, and he liked the way the woman looked at him—full on, but unstaring. He smiled back at her. "I am Otto. I don't speak English bery well."

"Why, honey, you sound fine to me! Where you from?"

Paula had coached him thoroughly on this point. "Brazil. I visit my cousins."

"That's nice. You like it here in Texas?"

"Yes, ma'am." Unfamiliar trees and houses flowed past the huge windows. He pulled the words he wanted out of the back of his throat. "It is very strange. I get—homesick."

"I bet you do, but don't you give in to that." She had a forceful, bright way of speaking that was heartening even while her words didn't seem to fit together. "You going downtown to see the Alamo?"

"What's thalano?"

"Heavens, don't you know about that?" The lady's eyes lit up with a peculiar fire, like Mr. Feinman's when he talked about music. "Why, I'm ashamed of your cousins! That's just about the finest thing that ever happened!"

Ahto did not catch every word of the story she told him, but her manner of telling what he did understand stirred his blood. Apparently a great battle had taken place here once, with two hundred men dying rather than surrendering to the evil soldier, Santa Anna. Ahto liked Davy Crockett best, because he was sort of a priest, singing to cheer the besieged. Unfortunately, the woman didn't know any of the songs Crockett had sung. He told her about the battle of Narrow Pass, in return, and she was encouragingly interested.

"Then you know just how we feel about the Alamo," she said. "A lot of people laugh at us for bragging on it, but that's just because their cities don't have anything to match it. Oh, here comes my stop. Could you ring the bell for me? Just push that little black strip."

Heartened by the success of this encounter, Ahto spent the rest of the trip looking out the window at a bewildering assortment of passing scenes and smiling bravely at the people who stared at him. After all, his great-grandparents hadn't been afraid of the lowland army. Why should he be afraid of rude people?

The driver let him off on a concrete corner, full of people. The first thing he noticed were the buildings. Ahto had resigned himself to a world full of boxes, but suddenly everywhere he looked were decorative moldings and odd shapes. The very hugeness of so many of these houses was subtly comforting—he no longer felt exposed on all sides, with these fantastic edifices soaring above him. He set off at random, crossing the street with a bunch of grown-ups who walked defiantly under the noses of a row of impatient cars.

Soon he came to a place where the street was railed. Curious, he looked through and found himself peering into a channel of greenish brown water, its banks green with unblooming plants where they weren't taken up by broad sidewalks. Above rose a building, unimaginably high, from which carved stone faces looked cheerfully down. Every few yards trees arose, the tallest he had seen since coming here, their roots on the riverbank. A bright orange barge, with no apparent means of propulsion, passed below the street. On his left, a staircase curved down from the street level. The old woman had mentioned a river. Santa Anna had lost so many soldiers and so much time, he hadn't bothered to bury them all, but had tossed them in the river and run off after General Houston. The pleasant channel below him had been clogged with carrion. Ahto descended into the smell of green water and a trapped, morning chill.

He wandered for some time, smiling at people and staring at new sights, comfortably closed in and anonymous. When he got hungry, after some hesitation, he stopped a young woman who smiled at him and got directions to a place that would sell him food without using up all his money. The people there were quite helpful, once he admitted that he couldn't read the list of meals on the chalkboard outside the door. Tucked into a dim corner inside, where he would attract a minimum of stares, he ate a huge sausage with onions and mustard and drank milk. Water chattered loudly, tumbling over man-made falls and aqueducts, spraying ferns and other greenery with fine mist. Tables were set out on the broad sidewalk, chairs arranged invitingly around them, and warm smells challenged the coolness of the river. It was all very pleasant, but Ahto was worried. He had less than three dollars left. Assuming all meals cost about the same, he could eat supper tonight, and then he would have to either go home or find out where money came from.

Would he even be welcome at home? Mr. Feinman would be back sooner or later. Even if Aunt Sally and Paula didn't want him anymore, Mr. Feinman would.

The thought of Aunt Sally and Paula not wanting him made him feel hollow inside. That morning he wouldn't have been able to imagine it, but that morning he hadn't met Tom. Who was he? Was he going to stay? Why was Aunt Sally so mad at Tom? Maybe he should go straight to Mr. Feinman's house and get answers before attempting to go home.

As long as he was down here, he might as well see the Alamo. He followed directions again, this time the waiter's, coming up off the river into an open space not resembling a battlefield at all. A huge white monument stood in the middle, and the area was surrounded by more fancy buildings and asphalt streets. Across the way was a low building with a scrolled top, which he remembered seeing in a picture on the wall in Ms. Bingham's room. He assumed that this must be the Alamo.

Despite his worries, Ahto enjoyed that afternoon. The Alamo had quiet grounds to walk in, and inside the buildings there were so many things to look at that his head swam—relics of the soldiers, flags, pictures, a model of the way the battle had looked. He wanted to see the instrument Crockett had played, but no one seemed to know where to find it. Maybe Santa Anna had smashed it. After he had seen everything there, he went out again and wandered randomly through a world so strange he felt oddly comfortable. Plenty of other people looked just as lost as he was, and he saw more than one person who lacked something most of the others had. One man had only one arm, and he accidentally walked into a woman who couldn't see, who had been stepping along confidently with a cane. One girl, thin like him, was in a wheeled chair, apparently unable to move without it. Next to such differences, what was a finger or nose more or less?

Ahto walked till he was exhausted and completely turned around among low, yardless buildings. If he looked over his shoulder he could still see the huge, top-heavy column one grown-up had pointed out to him—"If you can see the Tower of the Americas, you're not lost." If he walked toward it, he would get back downtown, but what would he do then? His feet hurt, and his head was light despite its burden of questions.

Just as he sat down to rest on the curb, a man with a picture of a cat on his arm came out of a nearby doorway. His sleeve was rolled up so that he could admire the orange-and-black stripes rippling with the movements of his muscles. Ahto sat up straight. Enough people had commented on the tattoos on his hands that he knew the English word, but he had never before seen a native possessing one. He forgot to be nervous. "Excuse me, sir. Where did you get that tattoo?"

The young man took a moment to answer. Ahto was used to this by now. "Right here," he said, jerking his thumb over his shoulder. "Beaut, ain't it?"

"Yes, sir," said Ahto uncomprehendingly, and watched him go out of sight. Opening his hands, he examined his palms. The red feather on the right had been there since the day his father had named him; it might as well have been born on him. Every day of his life, it was there to remind him that he was a priest, the son of a priest, the servant of the World Bird. The red circle on his left hand had been there almost as long, since he'd learned to walk, announcing his right to feed the sacred birds, his duty to learn to read and sing, as well as herd and hunt and handle a knife like other boys. In their way, they were good markings, an identity he could close his fist on; but they were baby marks. What he needed now was a red bird, flying across his chest, and then he would be entitled to flute lessons, public singing, and proper healing and chanting lessons. Not that anyone here could teach him the proper chants, but Renay was taking flute lessons at school. He could sing in the choir, if he had the right tattoo.

I'm old enough, he thought crossly. I ought to have it. He looked at the dusty glass door and fingered the money in his jeans pocket. "It won't hurt to ask," he said aloud. Resolutely he strode through the door.

CHAPTER 9

Lifestage

A bell jangled discordantly as he entered an interior of cold fluorescent light and rank smoke. A dark brown man was leisurely inserting a drawing of a heart under the skin of a man on a stool. An ancient, dark brown woman, like a heap of rope behind the cash register, breathed deeply at a darker brown cigarette.

All Ahto's speech went out of him when she looked up. Her eyes peered into and through him, as if examining every fault on his conscience, every unrecognized virtue in his soul. The eldest priest had looked at him like that shortly before he'd died, and Ahto had woken from dreams of it for weeks. Gray, choking smoke drifted into his nostrils. I'm supposed to say hello now, he thought; but the impudence of speaking uninvited to those eyes overwhelmed him, and he stood before her, waiting.

She leaned over the cash register and turned over his right hand; nodded; turned over the left. Ahto swallowed. She fixed her eyes on his again. "How old are you?"

"Ten," he croaked.

"You need a tattoo?"

"Y-yes, ma'am. A red bird. Flying. Right here." He laid his hand upon his chest.

The old woman released his eyes, sketching quickly on a pad at her elbow. "Like that?"

Ahto did not wonder how she had gotten so close on the first try. "The beak should be hooked more. And three spread feathers on this wing. Yes, ma'am. Like that."

"I can do that. Go sit on that stool."

Ahto obeyed, his heart beating so hard he could swear it was shaking his body. The other tattoo artist paused in his work to say something rapid about *niños*. "It's all right for this child," she answered. Only now did Ahto realize that she had been speaking Spanish all along.

He watched her arrange her equipment. "Take off your shirt," she said. "What's your name?"

"Ahto." He knew who she was now, but swallowed and asked, in his own language: "Are you—is your name Rose?"

She looked at him with eyes as deep as the world. "Obviously."

Ahto squirmed. "I don't mean to be stupid. Only everything's so confusing. You—you used to know my grandmother. Talira."

Rose smiled and set about her work. Ahto sat submissive, feeling vaguely that she must be a dream, come to get him while awake. It did not surprise him that she asked no grown-up questions—what he was doing here, how his grandmother was. Such interests were for ordinary people. "You ought to be singing," she said; so he sang softly, as much as he knew of the proper song. The other tattooer said something in Spanish. Rose told him to shut up.

At last Rose sat back, surveyed her handiwork, and said, "There. Take a look." Ahto swiveled his stool to face the mirror. The soaring bird was shockingly red against the paleness of his chest, just like his father's. Despite all his efforts to maintain an adult dignity, his mouth kept trying to grin, and happiness bubbled inside him like Coke in a glass.

When he tried to pay her, she just shook her head. "You don't pay for that tattoo," she said. "That's your right. Better get on home now. It's getting late."

Ahto shifted uncomfortably. "I'm not sure I want to go home."

"How come?"

Rose listened with still, bright eyes as he explained about being a tattletale and about Tom.

"I wouldn't worry about that Tom person," she said. "Sounds to me like he and Aunt Sally were married, and aren't anymore."

"But you can't stop being married!"

"You can around here. He won't even stay overnight, if Aunt Sally has any sense."

"But what about Paula?"

"She was the one did wrong. If she's your friend, she'll make up. Get along home now. We're going to close. Say hello to Father Raven for me."

"How did you know about Father Raven?"

Rose laughed and lit another cigarette. "When you're as old as me, you'll know everything, too."

Ahto had trouble finding the right bus, but the drivers were helpful. Darkness had fallen by the time he reached Woodlawn Lake. He was hungry, and a little nervous, planning what he should say as he walked around the broad expanse of water. As he approached, he saw that the house was all lit up and surrounded by cars: Aunt Sally's, Nana's, Tom's, and Mr. Feinman's. Ahto hesitated on the sidewalk.

The curtains of Paula's window parted, and her silhouette stood sharp against electric light. He heard the rasp of the window rising. "Paula?" he called softly. "Paula! I'm sorry I was a tattletale!"

"Ahto?" He was relieved at the sound of her voice. "I was just going to sneak out and look for you. I'm sorrier than you are. I should've told Daddy to bring you, too, only I was being mean. Come inside quick! Everybody's downstairs arguing about what to do to find you."

Relieved of the weight of several large stones in his stomach, Ahto went in. The hall was too bright and warm after the chill evening. A smell of steak twisted his empty stomach. The first thing he heard was angry adult voices; the second was Paula thundering downstairs, calling: "He's back! He came back, y'all!"

Steeling himself for the onslaught, Ahto unbuttoned his shirt so everyone could see the tattoo, marched into the living room, walked straight up to Mr. Feinman, and got his news out before the tide of grown-up reactions swept over him.

"I can sing in the choir now," he announced. "And I want to learn the flute."

Paula lay in bed, staring at the window. Below, she could hear the murmur of voices through the floor vent—her father talking to her mother. She didn't like to think about her father, now that he was here. It was all her fault that they had left Ahto behind this morning, of course. He couldn't be blamed for that. All the same, she didn't want to think about him, didn't like the uneasy sensation she got when she did. His voice— Mama's voice—gibberish, drifting through the vent.

Flesh and blood can only bear so much. Half an hour after her good-night kisses, Paula rose and crouched near the vent. From this angle she could see only wallpaper and an empty couch, crossed occasionally by her father's restlessly pacing shadow.

"I don't see why you had to keep him here."

"I don't see what business it is of yours."

"Sally, he's living with my kids. My kids are my business."

"Then tend to business more often! Those Christmas presents were nearly three months late, in case you lost count. You never so much as called—"

"Don't change the subject!"

"Otto isn't the issue here, Tom. Your behavior—"

"How can you say he isn't the issue? You moved a tattooed freak into the same house as our kids—"

Paula lay very still, wishing she had stayed in bed.

"Don't call him a freak. Especially don't let Paula hear you call him that. He's an extremely bright, talented little boy."

"Yeah? Then why can't he speak English?"

"He speaks better English after two months than you spoke Spanish after two years. Obviously, whoever took care of him before wasn't educating him. Between us, Mama and Earl and I—"

"And that's another thing! Who's this Earl person? We come home, Paula has a crisis, won't even tell me what's wrong, but she straightaway calls the music teacher. What's the music teacher got to do with anything? How long has he been hanging around?"

A cold pause. Paula wished—no, she didn't. She was glad Daddy had come to see them. She was glad she had found Ahto. She couldn't put her finger on the problem, couldn't figure out what she needed to wish.

"Tom. Go away. Next time you feel like seeing the kids, call first."

"You haven't answered me."

"I don't have to. Get out."

Daddy's shadow stopped pacing, casting darkness

over the cheerful yellow pattern of the wall. "I'm sorry, Sally. Everything's gone weird on me. None of this has been what I planned at all."

"Nothing ever is."

"Look. I've got a job up in Austin. I'll come see the kids more often. I'll call."

"I'll believe that when I see it."

"Give me a break!"

"I've given you breaks, Tom. I'm as broken as I'm going to get. Now get out of my house."

"Your mother's house."

"Don't nitpick. If she had her way, you'd never've been allowed in. Tom, I'm tired. I want you to go away, and I want to go upstairs to my nice, wide, empty bed, and sleep."

"All right. But things will change, Sally. Wait and see."

Feeling old and tired, Paula watched the lights of his car drive away and curled up in bed, waiting to cry.

CHAPTER **10**

The Broken Bird

"**I**mmortal, invisible, God only wise," Ahto sang, a little breathlessly, as he pumped the secondhand bike along. "In light inaccessible hid from our eyes."

The light this morning was anything but inaccessible. Ahto's cheeks were sore with sunburn gained at recess during the past week. Spring didn't waste any time on misty, rainy days here in San Antonio.

"You look like a duck in that hat," Peter called over his shoulder.

Ahto pulled the brim of his baseball cap down to cut off more of the early, eye-punching light. "Quack," he said.

"I wish you were a duck, Ahto!" said Paula. "Ducks can at least peck back when they're hit."

"Paula got detention, Paula got detention," crowed Peter.

"Shut up, Peter," said Ahto automatically. "I didn't mean for you to get in trouble. Priests are supposed to sing and heal people and take care of birds and stay out of fights."

"You were in a fight as soon as he pushed you. Anyway, you can't be a priest here. Only grown-ups are priests." Ahto had explained about serving the World Bird as best he could, but he didn't think she had really gotten the point. "Peter, you stop for that sign, or if the car doesn't wallop you, I will!"

Ahto sighed. Generally, these morning rides through the burgeoning world were pleasantly full of bird song, flowers, and low-lying sunbeams. Uneasiness generally held off until he was in sight of school, but today she had reminded him, and the relentless gnaw in his stomach set in early. What terrible thing would happen today? His cap stolen and tossed from boy to boy? Some mark of attention from Mr. Feinman, bringing upon his head the dreadful murmur of "teacher's pet"? Being ignored by Ms. Holubek when he raised his hand, and called on when he didn't? Paula rescuing him from Dan's clutches again, repeating her detention-earning feat of kicking him in the face? Or some new, unimagined horror?

He remained in suspense until recess, at which time he conscientiously attempted to play dodgeball while Paula attended Amy's club. Ahto didn't understand about this club, but it seemed important for Paula to be part of it, and boys were not allowed. This left him with the necessity of acting as much like a local boy as possible. He was getting rather good at dodgeball, but he could tell something was going to go wrong today when Dan came and stood with his hands in his pockets, watching. Kyle threw fast and furiously. Ahto, distracted, narrowly escaped being tagged by leaping jerkily sideways.

"Lookit him," sneered Dan. "Think he'd never seen a ball before, the sissy."

"Lay off," said Kyle, hitting the ball on the rebound so that it smashed into the wall just too late to tag Renay's arm. "Nobody asked you to play."

"I wouldn't play with a sissy like him, anyway."

"He's not a big enough sissy to fight with girls," said Roy. Dan glowered. The ball caught Roy on the hip.

To Ahto's relief, Dan moved on, pausing to annoy Amy's club—a cluster of six girls nattering in the shade. Ahto, distracted by anxiety for Paula, became "it" almost immediately, but as he took his place, he saw Joe Santos approaching and returned his concentration to the game. The club was safe for now. Joe was the biggest boy in school, having been held back twice. Ahto counted him among the people he needed to dread, but Joe's little sister, Janie, was part of the club, almost as important to it as Amy. Nobody picked on Janie when Joe was around, and the protection extended to her friends.

The afternoon was muggy and draining, but Ahto—inspired by Dan's scorn—played hard until he could hardly tell up from down. When the ball hit him in the face, he was completely unprepared and went down like a rodent before a slingshot. For a moment he only lay, blinking in darkness, as voices shrilled unintelligibly above him. Someone helped him to his feet, and he followed where he was led, through a world gone nauseating. The light hurt as much as the aftershock of the ball. When the people leading him eased him onto the grass in the shade, he lay still, trying to make shapes out of colors, words out of voices.

". . . s'matter, sissy couldn't . . ."

". . . teacher's coming . . ."

"What'd you . . ."

". . . such a worrywart."

"Never mind that baby. Look what I got."

Frightened cheeping pierced the roaring in Ahto's ears.

"Joe, leave it alone."

"Why should I?"

"Otto? Otto? You all right?"

"Ahto, say something!"

Cheep, cheep! Wings fluttered. Someone was doing something to a bird. Ahto tried to find which direction was up so he could sit.

"Hey, let me see."

"Lie still, Ahto."

"Ooh, gross. He looks like he's dead and the rats've been chewing on him."

Cheep! Cheep!

"He's a zombie. He's trying to get up."

94

"Ahto, just lie still."

Ahto did not see Paula's face, because he wasn't looking for it. He found himself pushing through a forest of bodies to find the sight of Joe and Dan bent over a feathered shape in Joe's hand. Dan poked it with a stick. It fluttered feebly.

"Leave it alone," croaked Ahto, with a rubbery, uncooperative mouth.

Joe stretched a wing to its full length, grasping the fledgling tighter as it struggled. "Leave it alone!" said Ahto clearly.

Joe looked at Ahto and laughed, stretching the wing just a little farther. "Who's going to make me?"

"What are they doing to that poor bird?" asked Amy.

"Leave it alone!" said Ahto. His voice felt thick and sounded too loud and too shrill. "He never did anything to you."

Dan poked with his stick. The fledgling struggled futilely. Joe laughed again.

Ahto hit Dan in the face, bit one of Joe's hands, and twisted the other. Then he was holding the soft, fluttering, panicked creature close to his chest, bent all around that point of fear, taking blows passively on his back, head, shoulders—everyplace but on the bird. The world was noisy around him. Paula's battle cry rang clear and strong, unsilenceable even through the teacher's whistle.

Ms. Bingham hauled Ahto to his feet and scattered her look of authority as if it were feed corn. "What's this about?" she demanded, from about a hundred miles away.

"He hit me," declared Dan virtuously.

"And bit me," added Joe.

Ahto was too busy calming the fledgling to answer. His legs did not want to hold him, so he sat down. People kept talking and arguing above him. "His wing's broken!" he exclaimed in dismay.

Ms. Bingham's face went soft as he showed her, then stern again, as she looked at Dan and Joe. "Is this true?"

"We didn't do nothing to it," said Joe sulkily.

"Liar!" said Paula. "He was pulling its wing off, and Dan was hitting it with that stick."

Accusations flew through air. Ahto hummed a healing song, trying desperately to remember what his father had said about broken wings. Someone patted his shoulder. He looked up, the motion of his head making him feel sick again.

"I think this calls for a little trip to the principal's office," said Ms. Bingham.

This trip was tedious and anxiety ridden. The existence and injury of the bird exonerated Ahto of all but the most minor transgression, but they insisted on asking all sorts of questions about his blackout before letting him tend the wing. Then they tried to tell him the bird was hurt beyond repair and should be "put out of its misery"—by which they meant killed.

"I can fix it," he insisted. "I fixed lots of them at

home. And I'm just fine." This was essentially true. The terrible faintness had mostly passed, now that he was out of the sun. He had brought up a lot of fallen fledglings and mended lots of wings, or assisted, as part of his preparation for the priesthood. This would be the first time, however, that he had to deal with *both* problems at once.

Fortunately, the sixth-grade science teacher—Mr. Rodriguez, who was much nicer than Ms. Holubek—happened along on entirely different business and agreed to help him, providing a nest box and wing-splinting materials out of a closet full of mysterious paraphernalia in the back of his classroom.

"You mustn't expect it to fly, though," cautioned Mr. Rodriguez. "Its bones are still growing, and if everything isn't just right they may grow wrong. And even if you do everything possible, it may die anyway."

"I got to try," Ahto said.

Mr. Rodriguez nodded, just as if he understood. "Of course you do."

All through the time he should have been in music class, Ahto sat alone in an empty classroom and crooned healing songs to the broken bird. Remembering that birds had to eat almost constantly at this age, he scrounged in his and Paula's lunch boxes and along the windowsills to see what the bird would eat. Dead flies and apple core were best received. This healing would be dauntingly difficult without his father and the resources of the village aviary. In his head Ahto made a

97

list of the things he would need. The time seemed short before the class returned noisily for study hall and gravitated toward him.

"Otto got Joe into trouble," hissed Janie.

Ahto was silent. Janie and Amy were the most important girls in the fifth grade. Paula had to really work to stay in the club, and he didn't want to make life hard for her. However, she seemed determined, as usual, to make life hard on herself.

"Joe got himself into trouble," said Paula. "It's not Ahto's fault Joe and Dan picked on a poor defenseless bird."

"He didn't have to bite him," said Janie haughtily.

"You got the bird in there?" asked Kyle, coming to hover over the box. "Can I see it?"

Ahto found himself, as usual, the center of a group of faces—but, unusually, more of them were curious than hostile, and most of them had their eyes fixed on the box, not on his face. His mouth was dry, awaiting harsh words, as he said: "I can show people one at a time. If you all crowd around you'll scare him."

"Who wants to look at a dumb old bird?" sneered Janie.

"Yeah," said Carla Gross, another fringe member of the group.

Amy leaned forward hesitantly, looked at Janie.

"I'm sure we're all interested in Otto's bird," said Ms. Bingham, disrupting the crowd's cohesion with her teacher smile, "but that's not what study hall's for. Besides, I'm sure the poor thing's been through enough today. Suppose you let me keep it at my desk till after school, Otto. I promise no one will disturb it."

"Paula's cat will eat it," pronounced Amy decisively.

"No she won't. I won't let her," said Ahto, turning the box over to Ms. Bingham reluctantly. "He needs to be fed a lot," he informed her. "Apple core and flies."

"Gross," said Carla.

"Don't talk about yourself," said Kyle rudely.

Ahto looked around the room and had the sense of patterns shifting.

The Fledgling Fighters

The cafeteria arrangement had settled down into a comfortable norm that accommodated both Ahto's peculiar position and the school mores. The club—Amy Rimbaum, Janie Santos, Julie Pickthorn, Nancy Reyes, Carla Gross, and Paula—clustered around one end of a long table. Ahto sat within a seat or two of Paula, and whatever boys had reason to be there that day—Kyle, Renay, and Roy, for sure—clustered on the other side of him. This kept both groups from the odium of sitting with the opposite sex, while leaving them intact, connected by the practical inseparability of Paula and Ahto.

The day after the bird incident, they came to the table as usual. Janie, Carla, and Nancy were already seated at one end, Roy and Kyle at the other. Paula put her tray next to Carla's while Ahto took his place two seats away, opposite Roy. Janie fixed him with a cold glare, stood up with a deliberate rattle of her chair, and went to the next table, where she banged her tray down and presented them with a stiff back.

Carla and Nancy stopped eating. Paula looked after her. "Janie? What's the matter?"

"I've sat at the same table with that long enough," said Janie loudly, without turning around.

Paula's stomach sank even as her anger rose. "With what? At the same table with what?"

Janie turned dramatically, pointing an accusing finger at Ahto. "With that!"

Glances ran around the table. Nancy's mouth set in a stubborn line. Carla looked at her hands, took her tray, and sat down next to Janie. No one said anything. Amy and Julie were crossing the room.

Amy looked the situation over with a blank face. Julie looked at Janie's back, Ahto's bowed head, Nancy's mouth, and then at Amy. Paula forgot to breathe. "What's going on?" asked Amy. "Why is Janie over there?"

"Because she's still mad at Ahto," answered Nancy, before Paula could get around the choking sensation in her throat.

Amy looked from Janie's stiff back to Paula's face. Paula had never seen her hesitate like this before. Ahto conscientiously ate his meat loaf. "Come on, Janie," Amy said. "Don't be mad."

"He bit my brother." Janie forced each word out of her mouth as if it were a rock, aimed and thrown.

"Your brother was torturing a poor little bird," said Paula, her eyes on Amy's face. She knew very well why she was in the club with the two most important girls in the fifth grade. As long as Amy liked her, then the other girls would like her, too. It was that simple.

"That doesn't mean Otto can bite just whoever he feels like," said Janie.

"Well, that's true." The expression on Amy's face was unfamiliar. Paula's stomach hurt with suspense. "Maybe if he said he was sorry—"

Ahto looked up, his eyes round and pale. Paula shook her head sharply. It would be just like him!

"That's dumb," said Renay, breaking the silence at the boys' end of the table. "Joe picked on a bird and beat Otto up, and he never said he was sorry. Who cares where that dumb girl sits?"

"I don't see why he should have to say he's sorry if Joe doesn't," Paula said quickly. She wished Renay hadn't gotten his words out first. "And I don't see why you can't sit at the same table as your friends. Don't be silly."

"Anybody that's friends with Otto isn't friends with me," declared Janie.

"Then you're not a very good friend to have anyway," said Nancy. "Y'all can sit over there and be stuck up if you want to. We don't need you."

"You're still my best friend, aren't you?" said Amy, unexpectedly plaintive, to the back of Janie's head.

"Not if you're friends with Otto and Paula," said Janie implacably.

Amy looked once around the table, carried her tray five feet farther, and sat down at Janie's right hand.

Paula began determinedly to shovel down her peas and carrots. She hated peas and carrots.

Julie stood, blank-faced. Paula did not look at her.

"So can we come look at the bird today after school?" asked Kyle.

"I'm building a cage," said Ahto.

Julie went to sit next to Ms. Bingham.

"Janie's a pig anyway," said Nancy confidentially. "My mama says people who're cruel to animals are the lowest form of life on earth."

"That's right," said Paula, wanting to cry. "They grow up to be terrorists and things."

She went around in a daze for the rest of the day, watching the fifth grade fall out along the new lines. Most people sided with Amy and Janie, of course, but Paula was surprised by the number who didn't—who either hovered indecisively, like Julie, or came out in open rebellion. Paula had never cared much about Nancy before, one way or another, but today she was invaluable. To this girl, at any rate, the question was not one of popularity, but of principle—either you approved of cruelty to animals or you sided with Paula.

The third day after the fight, Julie came to eat lunch with Nancy and Paula. The other three members of the disrupted club sat ostentatiously at the next table discussing Carla's birthday party for next week, which would be their first chance to snub the defectors. Kyle and Renay talked about baseball.

"Those girls are such creeps," said Julie.

Ahto looked over, his flat face wearing its troubled expression. "I'm sorry I made y'all so much trouble," said Ahto. "I couldn't help it."

"Of course you couldn't," said Paula. "We don't care about any dumb birthday party." By this time, she really didn't.

"That's right," said Nancy stoutly. "My mama said we can have a slumber party for Cinco de Mayo."

"What's Cinco de Mayo?" asked Ahto.

Paula met Amy's eyes over the intervening heads as Nancy and Renay explained about the Mexican holiday. She set her mouth and lifted her chin.

Amy looked away.

CHAPTER **12**

The Mending

During the next few weeks, Ahto practically lived on the back porch. Nana would not allow him to bring the bird indoors, so his savings—accumulated because he didn't understand enough about things to buy much— were plundered for chicken wire to enclose one end of the porch, where the bird could exercise and Ahto could take care of him. Ahto sang the old bird-tending songs as he saw to the wing and set out bowls of sugar to attract bugs the fledgling could catch himself.

Carmen soon learned to run away whenever any- one approached; but no one was home from eight to three forty-five on weekdays, and her cat door did not keep her in. Ahto worried about this, until one day he came home with Kyle to find Father Raven sitting on the back-porch railing, the fledgling stuffing himself with ants, and Carmen on the back step ignoring both of them. Ahto hadn't seen Father Raven, except at a distance, for months. He forgot that Paula had told him not to speak his own language in front of other people, and greeted the bird politely.

"Thank you, Father Raven. You are most kind."

"Prrt," laughed the bird, pecking under his wing. "I just like to pick on cats. I'm too big to catch, and she knows it. See you." He flew off with a rattle of wings before Ahto could ask him how he was doing.

Kyle looked after the raven's flight. "Were you talking to him?"

"Uh—sort of," said Ahto, kneeling in front of the cage and opening his lunch box for the leftovers inside.

"You're pretty weird," said Kyle not unkindly, getting down next to him. "Anybody'd think you could understand birds, like Dr. Dolittle or something,"

Ahto opened the door of the enclosure. "Who's Dr. Dolittle?"

"Oh, come on! Doesn't anybody in Brazil know anything?"

The fledgling hopped up to peck at the peach pit in Ahto's hand. Kyle explained about the famous books in which a man learned to speak animal languages. The sun was warm and still on the lawn.

Ahto listened to Kyle with part of his brain, but the other part was thinking about the change that had come over his life. Suddenly boys were coming to visit him at home, and no one was picking on him except Dan and Joe. No one had shoved him in the hall or stolen his baseball cap for two weeks now. Boys who had sneered at him said "Hi" when they passed him in the hall; those who had ignored him asked how was he and would he like to play softball; and those who had good-naturedly stood by him—Kyle, Roy, and Renay—had become his best friends. His music lessons suffered somewhat, for he no longer had entire weekends free, but Mr. Feinman seemed positively pleased about this, and there was certainly a lot to be said for spending Saturday afternoons in backyards with other boys.

"I could lend a couple to you," said Kyle. "But you'd have to be careful. They're really my mom's, and she's had them since she was little."

"I'd like to read them," said Ahto. "But you know I don't read so well."

"You need to practice. I could help you."

"I would like that," said Ahto.

Paula and Ahto stretched on their bellies on the back porch, watching the bird gobble ants out of the sugar saucer. He was improving rapidly, gaining new feathers every day. "Nana says he's going to be a mockingbird," said Paula.

"It would begin with an *m*." Ahto sighed.

"You can say *m*'s real good now."

"Only when I think about it." He touched the face of the book Kyle had lent him, *Dr. Dolittle and the Green Canary,* and his own face brightened. "I almost finished this. I'm reading almost every word."

An uncomfortable thought occurred to Paula.

107

"You know, as well as you're doing, the grown-ups are going to feel safe asking where you came from pretty soon. What you going to tell them?"

He looked at her with those perpetually astonished eyes. "The truth, of course."

"But they won't believe you. They'll think you're telling stories. Or crazy." Her heart began stepping lively. "If they think you're crazy, they'll put you away. Lock you up with people who really are crazy."

"Would Aunt Sally do that?"

Paula thought a minute. "If she thought it was the best thing to do for you."

"I wouldn't like that," said Ahto slowly, watching the mockingbird.

Paula had largely gotten used to Ahto, but every now and again—like now—she looked at him and knew again that he was magical, irreplaceable. She tried to think how someone in a book or on TV would handle this. "Hey, I've got an idea," she said, eventually. "Pretend you got amnesia."

"An-ne-?"

"Amnesia. That's when you get a bump on the head and lose your memory." Paula had seen lots of TV plots revolving around amnesia, and spoke with confidence. "Sometimes it goes away by itself, and sometimes you need another bump on the head. They'll leave you alone, because it'd make it worse to worry you about it."

A male cardinal called from a branch of magnolia. The mockingbird raised his head, cocked his eye, and repeated the notes experimentally.

"Ahto, listen! He's learning to sing!"

Ahto nodded. "Father Raven says we need to start letting him out so he can learn to fly, too."

The big black bird was absent now, but Paula had grown used to seeing him around—a huge, cockeyed, rusty bird who seemed eternally on the verge of laughing at her. "He didn't really talk to you, did he?"

"Yes," said Ahto matter-of-factly. "We can understand each other, because we both came through the rift."

"Oh." Paula chewed over this. She had learned much of Ahto's history, in bits and pieces, during times like this. The thought of the rift between the worlds made hair stand up pleasantly along her arms. "I wonder if he was born in your world or mine?"

"I don't know. I can ask him."

"It might be rude." Paula frowned. Carmen, stretched along the porch rail, opened an eye and shut it again. "I wonder why cats don't go back and forth? I'm sure they're magic."

"They wouldn't be very welcome where I come from. Maybe they go someplace that has a World Cat. You wouldn't want Carmen wandering off and being lost a whole year, anyway."

"Is that how long it takes? How do you know?"

"Father Raven told me. Would you take Carmen inside and block up her door? I want to take the bird out."

Paula did so.

The last weeks of school dragged on, each one longer and hotter than the one before, with the exception of a spate of rain in May. Ahto took the bird out every day for exercise, even during the rain. Paula privately thought this would be bad for it, but whether through amazing luck (as Nana said) or Ahto's daily healing songs, the wing mended straight and true. Ahto got a *C+* for his book report on *Dr. Dolittle and the Green Canary*. Sometimes Nancy or Julie came over after school, and sometimes Paula went to their houses. Kyle, Renay, and Roy mostly came to the Luthers', to see the bird. When her father showed up for Peter's birthday, Paula was nervous, but all went well. He took them to the zoo again, this time including Ahto. The variety, number, and captivity of the birds seemed to sober and astonish him, but he didn't try to free them, as Paula had feared he might.

Shortly before school let out, Mr. Feinman and Aunt Sally, urged by Mr. Bottoms, began asking Ahto about his background. Under Paula's coaching, he persuaded them that he remembered nothing before his walk in the fog—though Paula and Ahto weren't positive he had fooled Aunt Sally or Mr. Feinman completely. Paula lay awake a few nights, worrying about how she had pushed him into lying to them—but grown-ups didn't believe in aliens. Not smart grown-ups, anyway. Once she had heard Nana and Mama discussing some people over in the rich part of town who claimed to have been visited by UFOs, and Mama had said that those who weren't actual liars were clearly too dumb to handle their own money. Ahto went in for a battery of tests, and one of the doctors recommended that he see a regular psychiatrist; but that threat ended after Mama sat up late one night with a calculator and her checkbook.

The last day of school arrived at last, and Paula stuffed all her notebooks into the top of the closet. "I'm going to read all I want to and go swimming every single day," she announced as she doled out the milk and cookies. "And Nancy's big brother promised to teach us to sail. You want to learn, too, Ahto?"

"I want to," said Peter through a mouthful of Oreo.

"What's sail?" asked Ahto.

"Oh—I'll show you. You'll like it." Paula dunked her cookie and regarded him compassionately. "I hope you'll have time. It's a real pain you're going to have to go to summer school."

"But I'll be able to read as well as you afterward," said Ahto. "Want to come see me let the mocking-bird out?"

Paula followed him onto the back porch. The bird, no longer a baby, waited impatiently, fluttering his white-patched wings and calling sweetly. Ahto put his milk and cookies on the floor and undid the latch, responding to the bird's cries with his own gentle sounds—whether birdcalls or words from his own language, Paula couldn't tell. Ahto was almost as tall as she was now, and his thin, tattooed hands moved surely. The door opened and the bird shot out without waiting for the hands to take him. He landed on the porch rail and sang the cardinal's song three times, so clearly and proudly that the cardinal sang back.

Where Carmen came from Paula didn't see, but she was there all right, and when the shocked cries, the waving hands, and the frantic winging subsided, she was there still, glowering indignantly under a lawn chair. The bird was high in the magnolia, aggressively flapping his white patches and screeching like a raven.

"You bad, bad cat!" Paula craned over the rail, measuring the distance from the ground to the branch with hopeless eyes. "You think we can get him down?"

"Did you see him?" Ahto asked in a proud, eager voice. "Did you see the way he flew? Like his wing'd never been busted at all!"

"But can we get him down again?"

The bird was calming somewhat, pecking his wings and sharply surveying the yard for more hidden threats.

"Why should we get him down?" asked Ahto. "He's well. I fixed him."

"But—don't you want to keep him?"

"Like in the zoo? What for?"

"Not like in the zoo. Like Carmen. For a pet."

"Birds aren't pets. They're—birds."

Paula watched the erstwhile fledgling edge along his perch. She remembered what Ahto had told her about the World Bird, how real birds were special to him—like angels or something. "What if he flies away? Won't you miss him?"

Ahto made a helpless, releasing gesture. "You don't keep birds."

A nasty thought struck Paula. "What if the boys at school won't like you anymore? What if they only liked you because of the bird?"

He blinked at her. "Are they like that?"

"I don't know. They might be. Amy was."

"If they are I won't like them anymore," declared Ahto firmly, adding: "I hope they're not. Roy and Kyle and Renay aren't, anyway."

"Chip, chip," said the mockingbird, and flew to the utility pole.

CHAPTER 13

Flu Season

Vacation ended, as usual, long before summer did, a fact Paula resented but was helpless to prevent. Ahto, having done well in summer school and been helped out of the irregularities of his registration by grown-ups, went into the sixth grade unhindered.

Over the hot summer days, Ahto had somehow been transmuted into a boy, rather than an alien. He swam at the Y, learned to sail, and was introduced by Kyle to softball and comic books. He might have always been around, like Peter, until something came up that he didn't know about.

"But why do we want to dress up like monsters?" he asked at lunch the week before Halloween.

"Because that's what it's about," said Julie. "The dead rise out of their graves and the witches have big parties and all the monsters come out. It's fun."

Ahto looked doubtful. "Nana says there are no monsters."

"Of course there aren't," said Renay scornfully. "Halloween is for gringos that don't know any better. El Día de los Muertos is the real thing. You go visit the graves of all your dead relatives, and you bring flowers and a picnic—"

"You don't have to be stuck up about it," said Kyle. "You go trick-or-treating same as the rest of us."

"This isn't helping Ahto understand any better," said Paula. "Look. A long time ago people believed that on this particular day the dead got up out of their graves and all that stuff Julie said. So they made a holiday to honor dead people—like a family reunion. That's what Renay's talking about."

"Only now we all know there's no such things as ghosts or witches," began Roy, but Renay interrupted him indignantly.

"My grandmother's a witch. Don't you tell me I don't have a grandmother."

"Your grandmother ain't either a witch."

"She is too! She's a *curandera*. You look in the Spanish-English dictionary, that's the same as a witch. She's the best *curandera* in town."

"She took my brother's warts off all right," Nancy chimed in.

"And she's got plants in her garden nobody else ever even heard of," added Renay.

"Well, but a *curandera* isn't the same as a witch,

115

whatever the dictionary says," said Paula, who had been reading up on the subject. "Witches are people who made a pact with the Devil, and she wouldn't do that."

"That's not witches, that's Satanists," said Roy. "That's just like another religion, only a nasty one."

So the discussion raged, and Paula was never sure that Ahto got to understand about Halloween. Nevertheless he made a convincing skeleton. On Peter's advice he did not wear a mask, but increased his natural pallor with Nana's powder puff and garnered awed compliments from strangers, as well as a prize at Amy Rimbaum's Halloween party. The entire sixth grade was invited to this affair. If hostility still existed between the fragments of the old club, no one could have known from watching. Paula even harbored a flickering hope that Amy would make up, but the night ended with mere politeness on both sides.

A norther kicked up, as if especially for Halloween night, carrying gray scuds of clouds along at a furious pace and biting through costumes and hidden sweaters to get at the flesh beneath. Ahto was astonished. "But it was hot this morning!" he protested, bending his powdered head into the blast as they worked their way up the street.

"Summer's over," answered Paula. "We've got to be cold once in a while."

"It could have warned us! We'll crack like one of those bottles in the science experiments."

"Ooh, we'd look really spooky then!" exclaimed Peter. "Our guts would all come out, and our heads would crack open so you could see the brains—"

"Shut up," said Paula.

Peter scurried ahead, butting against the norther like a goat in a United Federation of Planets uniform, singing in a voice that made Ahto wince noticeably:

"The worms crawl in and the worms crawl out.
They play pinochle on your snout. . . ."

The norther was still blowing spookily around the corners of the house when they returned after dark, as if it wanted to be a background for scary stories and hot chocolate. Ahto understood this part of the holiday well enough. He jumped clear off the floor when Mama pounced on him at the end of "The Golden Arm" and produced a few tales of his own, which he told with as much conviction as if he had met fog-wraiths himself. Mr. Feinman declared himself afraid to go home alone, lest he meet one.

Next morning Ahto came to breakfast looking as if the cold had indeed broken him like a bottle. His face was flushed, but he shivered inside his jersey, picking at his sausage and biscuits. Nana paused on her way around the table to feel his forehead. "You feel all right, baby?"

"My shoulders ache," said Ahto, "and my head, and my back."

"Lord, you're hot! Even for you. Paula, fetch me the thermometer."

"What did the doctor at Woodlawn Center say seemed to be normal temperature for him?" asked

Mama, as Paula hurried in and out of the bathroom. She remembered the ending of *The War of the Worlds*, when the Martians die of the common cold because they have no resistance to earth diseases. The idea made her uneasy.

"Ninety-nine point three, near as he could tell." Nana shook the mercury down. "Here, honey—hold that under your tongue."

Ahto obeyed listlessly.

"Maybe he should stay home," suggested Paula.

"I don't feel good either," declared Peter, drooping suddenly over the breakfast he had been bolting freely a moment before. "Maybe we should both stay home."

"Oh, you liar," said Paula matter-of-factly. "You're just fine. Even if you weren't, you could get better in a day or two, just lying in bed drinking juice. We don't know what to do for Ahto, he's so different from everybody else."

"Sometimes I wish you didn't read so much," said Mama. "I was hoping I'd be the only one to think of that. What's his temperature?"

Nana held the thermometer up. "One hundred and two. That's pretty high, even considering where he started from."

Ahto crouched miserably over his plate.

Paula could not concentrate that day. People in books were always getting deathly ill, wasting away with fevers, tossing in delirium. She had often wished she would get delirious—it sounded so exciting. But for Ahto to get sick and die, essentially alone in a strange world—the thought made her cold inside. It didn't help that no one else at school shared her concern, treating his absence as an ordinary ushering in of the flu season. Even Kyle thought she was overreacting when she spoke of the matter at lunch.

"Nobody ever died of the flu," he said. "Don't be such a worrywart."

"People have too," Paula protested. "I read a book once—"

"Just because it happened in a book doesn't make it true," interrupted Nancy. "You're always acting like the things you read are more important than things you've seen yourself. You don't know anybody who ever died of the flu, do you? They've got vaccines now."

"But what if they don't work on Ahto?"

"Why shouldn't they?" asked Renay. "He's human."

Paula stared into her mashed potatoes and succumbed to depression.

Kyle rode home with them. Nana was padding around the house in woolly slippers. "Whyn't you take this mustard plaster up? Save me a trip."

"Is he any worse?" asked Paula anxiously.

"You got to get worse before you get better," said Nana briskly. "He's drinking lots of juice. Reckon he'll be fine this time tomorrow. You got his homework there? You go on up, and make sure you bring the old mustard plaster back down with you."

"What's a mustard plaster?" asked Kyle as he and Paula climbed the stairs.

"A mess," answered Paula, handling the hot, damp cloth gingerly. "It's supposed to clear your chest. He must have a cough."

He did. The room smelled of sickness, mustard, and peppermint. Ahto lay in a welter of covers, an extra blanket and the old plaster slipping onto the floor. Paula tidied him up as Kyle hung back, abashed in the face of frailty. "Don't you let Nana catch you throwing mustard plasters on the floor," Paula said, trying to sound brisk, competent, and unconcerned. "How are you feeling?"

"All right," croaked Ahto, but red spots like bad makeup adorned his cheekbones, and his eyes were like dishwater. "Nana on't let ne lay the radio."

"You know you won't go to sleep if you're listening to music. You won't get well if you don't sleep."

"I on't get ell without nusic." The rim of his mouth was dry and stiff, robbing him of his hard-earned labials.

"I brought you your homework," said Kyle, setting the books and papers precariously on the edge of the nightstand among bottles and glasses. "There isn't much except for math."

Ahto blinked at him, as if he had forgotten how to understand him. The effort of paying attention to them was so visible they soon left him to himself and the silence. "He looks pretty awful for just having the flu," said Kyle on the front porch.

"I told you," said Paula. "He's made funny."

"Now would be a good time for him to remember

120

where his folks are. I bet they know all about it."

I bet they do, thought Paula as he rode away. If you could get through the fog and find them. The sky was gray and close above the housetops, but no fog drifted through the stillness—only the raven, high in the live oak, looked down and croaked dismally. Paula, feeling like a girl in a book, walked decorously over to stand beneath him. The bird was hard to see through the green leaves, but she turned her face toward him and tried to find some properly poetic words. "Father Raven? Father Raven?"

"Kark."

She had no poetry in her head at all. "Ahto's sick, Father Raven. I'm afraid he might die. Couldn't you bring him something to make him well, something from the other side of the fog?"

"Kark." A rattle of wings announced the hidden bird's departure. Oh, well. What had she expected? Only Ahto had enough magic in him to talk to birds.

Not even Mr. Feinman's evening visit roused Ahto's interest much; nor did he care about the beef bouillon Paula brought up for his supper. His skin was dry and white as notebook paper. "How did they take care of you when you were sick at home?" she asked.

"Ny ather sang to ne," he said, his eyes nearly closed, his mouth opening and closing like a beak. "Ny nother gave us rachik tea, and I heard healing songs. All healing is with songs." He leaned his head back on the twisted pillow and sang, hoarsely:

"A chi cu ru cu ru
A cha cu ru so—
A chi cu cu nulu
Chita culunu su do
Nara cu ru—"

A violent fit of coughing interrupted him and shook the bed.

"I'll make them give you some music," declared Paula, as if she could command and be obeyed. "I bet Mr. Feinman has some good records for sick people." She turned the radio on low, but all she got was a commercial for the American Dairy Association. Otto sang hoarsely across the jingle.

"Nara cu ru si dan
Cara no ru hostan—
Cara no chi si cron
Nara cu so dan—"

Paula was about to twist the dial when the DJ put on a record—ominously, about "the day the music died." She wasn't sure how well this would do in place of healing songs, but Ahto stopped singing and lay still.

She made him drink the last drops of bouillon and tiptoed downstairs, badly frightened. His voice hadn't sounded right at all.

Dinner was laid in the dining room, Mr. Feinman sitting between Peter and Mama, all of them waiting only for her. "Nana," she said, before her courage failed her, "please, let Ahto have some music. His daddy used to let him have music when he was sick."

"His daddy?" Mama and Mr. Feinman looked at her with the same half-eager, half-apprehensive expressions, but Mr. Feinman let Mama do the talking. "What'd he say about his daddy?"

Paula repeated the words as near as she could and glanced sideways at Nana over her pork chop. "I turned on the radio real soft for him. He wanted it bad."

"You shouldn't've done that after I'd said not to," said Nana.

"That's true," said Mama, "but you did say he hadn't slept all afternoon. Maybe the music will help. Let's let him have it till after supper and then we'll go check on him."

"Some people think music has healing properties," said Mr. Feinman. "What station is it?"

"The one that plays the oldies. He likes the classical station better, but you can't get it on that radio."

Paula remained thoughtful the rest of the evening, through dishes, Monopoly, and getting Peter to bed in Mama's room. Mr. Feinman, as happened sometimes, got into an involved grown-up conversation and was still in the living room when she came to kiss Mama and Nana good-night.

Paula lay awake a long time. She had been telling herself a story recently, every night, involving a heroine named Crystal (which was currently her favorite name) and a hero very like Ken in *My Friend Flicka* (which was currently her favorite book), and horses, and dra-

123

matic dangers, and deathly illnesses, and being lost in the Rocky Mountains with no grown-ups to help them out of their difficulties. For several weeks this story had been running, from high point to high point, carrying her off to sleep. Tonight it seemed simply silly. Ahto's music drifted across the hallway, Elvis Presley singing about blue suede shoes, and that was silly, too. She sat up and stared out the window, the ornamental lighthouse looming black against the gray cloud cover. Maybe it was her fault he was here. Maybe she had wished too hard for magic—maybe, by imagining the edge of the world outside her window that morning, she had actually created the edge over which Ahto had walked.

Carmen hopped onto the foot of the bed and stood kneading the soft springiness of the afghan. Paula lay down with her face next to her cat and asked hopelessly: "Carmen, what can I do?"

"Prr," said Carmen.

The light still shone in the hall. Grown-up voices came up the stairs and paused outside Ahto's room. "I hope we don't have to send him to the hospital," said Mama's voice. "I keep thinking—what if they won't take him?"

"If he were sick enough to send, they'd have to."

"I've heard of them turning away uninsured people. And he's not on my insurance. They won't let me put him on it at work without a lot of paperwork, which doesn't exist, of course."

"That's a point."

"And I'm afraid—what if they do take him and don't give him back? There must be an authority he falls under. The school hasn't reported him, and Woodlawn Center hasn't, but a hospital might. For his own good, or just because it's a rule."

"It wouldn't be for his good to take him away from you. Everybody's realized that so far."

"So far we've dealt with people, not organizations. Earl, we've got to find his parents. Sooner or later somebody'll take him away from us, and I don't want it to be a government agency."

"Well—but what else can we do? Put his picture on milk cartons?"

"I don't know . . ."

Their voices faded into the sickroom, under the sound of the news. Paula crawled back to the head of the bed in case Mama looked in on her way out, but they reemerged and passed her door.

". . . Brahms and so on," said Mr. Feinman.

"I hope it helps. If he's not better by Saturday, I'm taking him to a doctor."

A doctor. What did doctors know about interdimensional aliens? Could one really take him away? What if they gave him something wrong, something harmless to humans but deadly to aliens?

Paula passed an exceptionally bad night.

CHAPTER **14**

The Curandera Down the Street

By the time Paula came home from school the next day, Ahto was alternating between fitful sleep and restless, confused waking. He did not answer when spoken to, but produced those twittering, birdlike noises that had been all his speech when he first came. Mr. Feinman's albums did not seem to be helping, until they stopped. Then Ahto sat up in bed and called out, a piercing, frightened, meaningless noise like the distress of the baby mockingbird. Nana would not let Paula or Peter into his room anymore, but tiptoed in and out herself with mustard plasters, juice, soup, and aspirin. Peter walked around the house in his socks, trying to find some quiet amusement, and eventually settled on a jigsaw puzzle. Paula curled up on her bed with a book in her lap, staring out the window at a world bleak and cold, the lake a glittering gray mirror for the dull gray sky.

Mama made a doctor's appointment for the next afternoon.

Paula woke in the dark on Saturday morning and lay in bed as long as she could bear to. Then, dressing softly and leaving her bed unmade, she crept across the hall and opened the door, which was slightly ajar, just enough more that she could see in. The stereo had fallen silent, but the light indicating that the power was on glowed red in the dimness. Mama was huddled on Peter's bed, on top of the covers, her robe wrapped tight around her and her face unfamiliar in sleep—pale, slipping slightly sideways. It was hard to believe that mouth could make a stern line, or that forehead crease with concern. In contrast to her stillness, Ahto twisted in a tangle of covers, opened his eyes, and stared at Paula as if dumbfounded—his face a mask of angles, planes, and shadows. "Ahto?" whispered Paula.

"Chit suru ak!" said Ahto. "Suru! Suru! Suru!" A note of panic crept into his voice; he tried to sit up, and failed. Cold all over, Paula tiptoed away.

The hidden sun cast a slaty color into the sky beyond the YMCA. Paula stood on the front porch and listened to the stillness. After the close warmth of the house, the morning was fresh and cold. She stuffed her hands in her jeans pockets. Mama would take Ahto to the doctor today. After that—would they ever see him again? Would he die far away from everyone, or simply be sent to some orphanage? An orphanage would never let him out into the fog, thought Paula, looking at the lighthouse. He would never get home.

"Kark!"

Paula jumped. The raven landed on the porch rail not three feet away and cocked an eye at her intelligently. "Kark!"

"He's worse today, Father Raven," said Paula. "He doesn't recognize me."

"Kark!" Wings rattled as the raven launched himself across the yard, swooped low over the driveway, and landed on the handlebars of her bike, which she had abandoned hurriedly Friday afternoon and never gone back to put away. With an air of command, he spread his wings wide and said again: "Kark!"

"If this were a book," said Paula, "you'd lead me somewhere to something that would make him well."

"Prrt!" said Father Raven, as if laughing. Again he took off, circled the yard, and landed on the handlebars. She went toward him. When she was almost to the bike, he flew to the ground, head and tail cocked expectantly.

If Peter had been the one lying ill upstairs, Paula would have known that the raven's behavior was merely odd; now, she could not be certain that it was not also significant. She straddled the bike and met the bird's eye. "Well?"

"Prrt!" laughed Father Raven, hopping ahead of her down the driveway and rising, rising, flying toward the Y.

The longer Paula followed him, the more certain she was that he was leading her. He kept to the road, and when he got too far ahead he would circle back around, swooping low and croaking. The sky was pale blue and rose color before her, gray overhead and behind. They passed the deserted Y, its huge pool empty and forlorn. The houses beyond were shabby and quiet, full of people resting from their weekly early risings. Only the occasional lighted window announced the presence of someone pressed by necessity or habit to wake before the winter sun. The house upon whose roof Father Raven alighted was one of these—a small frame house, in need of paint, the yard cut up into plant beds. Paula leaned her bike against the wire fence and looked up at Father Raven. "Kark!" he challenged her.

Her stomach hurt as she pushed the gate open. What was she supposed to do? Knock on a perfect stranger's door and say a bird told her he might have something to cure the flu in aliens? The beady eyes dared her. Human shapes moved behind a paper blind. Paula knocked on the screen door.

In the winter morning stillness she heard the rustle of Spanish voices, feet upon a floor. Her mouth was dry and sore. The inner door opened.

"Oh, hi, Paula," said Renay. He looked surprised, embarrassed, and comfortably untidy, his hair uncombed, his feet stockinged. "Abuela says for you to come in."

"Uh—how did she know it was me?" Paula stepped in and he closed the door behind her. The house was cramped and stuffy, with the sharp odor of unfamiliar lives.

129

Renay shrugged. "She knew you were somebody."

"I didn't know you lived so close," said Paula, as he led her through a dark hall, stepping over a cat.

"Is Otto any better?"

"Worse. That's why I'm here."

The kitchen was bright and warm. Somewhere a shower ran; somewhere a radio played; but in here was only an old woman in a shapeless housedress, simultaneously mixing some kind of soup in a saucepan, boiling water in a kettle, and scrambling eggs with tortillas. Father Raven's silhouette stood against the window blind. The old woman turned and looked at Paula, a cigarette hanging carelessly from the corner of her mouth. The girl felt cold. She had never seen eyes like those, eyes buried in pits of brown wrinkles; eyes that peered into and through her, as if examining every fault on her conscience, every unrecognized virtue in her soul. So this was Renay's grandmother—the *curandera*. Gray smoke drifted into Paula's nostrils, and she choked.

"Uh—good morning, ma'am."

Without removing those disconcerting eyes from Paula's face, the *curandera* rapped out a sentence of Spanish. Renay replied in the same language. She nodded, turning the heat off under the kettle as it began to build toward a whistle, and said something else. Renay turned to Paula with the translation.

"She's going to give you some stuff that comes from the same place he does. You give it to him just whenever he wants it, like juice. It should work real

130

fast. If he's not better tomorrow, she'll make him something else."

"How does she know where he's from?"

"She knows a lot of things."

Wrinkled brown hands emptied the saucepan of
broth into a wide-mouthed Thermos and gave it to her
with a Ziploc bag of dried brown leaves, each as small
as a cat hair. "That's rachik tea," Renay translated.
"You make it just like ordinary tea. The soup isn't
exactly what his mother'd give him, but it's got most of
the right kind of stuff in it. She wants to know if he has
any music."

"Mr. Feinman brought some records over. Classi-
cals and church music—you know the kind of stuff
they like."

Renay repeated this in Spanish. His grandmother
nodded, those disconcerting eyes fixed upon Paula's
face. She tried to meet their gaze steadily, but didn't
feel that she succeeded. "She guesses that'll do. Nobody
around here knows the right songs."

The raven flew away as Paula put the Thermos into
her basket and tucked the Ziploc into her pocket. The
sun hovered just above the horizon, casting long, sharp
shadows down the street. "Does that bird come here
often?" Paula asked Renay.

"Sometimes," he said.

"He hangs around Ahto a lot."

Renay looked at her, and suddenly his familiar face
held an afterimage of his grandmother's transfixing
eyes. "You know where Otto really comes from, don't

you? You always knew he wasn't from Brazil or any place ordinary."

"Yes," said Paula. "He told me all about it. But I can't tell you, you know."

"I know. It's all right."

Paula got on her bike, curiosity struggling with shyness. It wasn't any business of hers. "Are you going to be a *curandera* too?"

"Curandero," he corrected. "Men are *curanderos.* I don't know. I'm working on it. By the time I'm grown up, maybe nobody'll believe in them anymore. Maybe I'll get hit by a car tomorrow and won't live to grow up. You can't plan that far ahead. I'm going to keep all her plants growing if I can, though. She's got lots of real useful plants."

This was the most coherent statement of philosophy Paula had ever heard from a boy other than Ahto. She rode home feeling comparatively young and frivolous. For Ahto to talk about his future duties as a maker of music and a servant of the World Bird was one thing; for a real boy, with a nose and hair, to talk calmly about not living to grow up was quite another. Avoiding cars and the image of her own skeleton in a short coffin, she hurried home and into the kitchen. Nana was cooking eggs and bacon while the pipes roared as they always did when someone took a shower.

"Goodness, Paula, what are you doing up and about so early?" asked Nana. "What's that you've got there?"

"I couldn't sleep worrying about Ahto," said Paula

truthfully. "Renay's grandmother sent these over. She says they'll help."

"Renay? Oh, that little Mexican friend of Otto's." Nana unscrewed the Thermos lid and sniffed thoughtfully, then eyed the bag of leaves. "What on earth is this?"

"Rachik tea. Ahto asked for it day before yesterday, but I didn't know what it was. He said his mother gave it to him."

"Did he? Never heard of it." Nana frowned. "I'd like to know what's in it, but I guess if he remembers it—and there's often good in those old recipes. Well, I'll make him some. Why not? The soup's a nice thought, anyway. It'll give him a change from bouillon."

If Paula expected some miraculous effect, she was disappointed. Nana had to hold the cup for Ahto, and when he lay down quietly afterward, it could just as well have been the Brahms on the stereo that calmed him as the tea. He drank it eagerly enough, however, and Nana was able to get a little of the soup inside him before he fell asleep.

Nana went to work, and Peter went down the street to play touch football, leaving Paula and Mama to clean house and check on Ahto periodically. Paula was still not allowed inside the room, but she could see that he was sleeping better; and when she looked in before lunch, he opened his eyes and saw her. "Aula?" he said, weakly. "An I late to school?"

"It's Saturday," said Paula. "How do you feel?"

"I'n hot," he complained, pushing off the covers he

133

had hitherto clutched so near. "I'n all sweaty."

"That means your fever's better. You want some more rachik tea?"

He blinked at her dully. "I didn't know you could get that here."

"Renay's grandmother had some."

Ahto rubbed his damp forehead as if trying to stimulate the circulation of thought. "Is her nane Rose?"

"I don't know. Father Raven took me to her."

"It nust be Rose." The conclusion seemed to give him some weary satisfaction. "I guess I should have sone nore. But it's so hot."

They brought him tea that steamed and juice that made the glass sweat. He drank both, listening to Mozart, and then fell asleep again. The down on his head was damp and dark; the papery whiteness of his skin softened into a healthier, milky shade. "He's better, isn't he?" asked Paula, setting the table for lunch.

"It looks that way," said Mama.

"Will you still take him to the doctor?"

"The appointment's already been made, and it's probably a good idea anyway. Don't look so scared. He's not going to the hospital or anything."

Ahto had to be helped out to the car, but he looked much better and could talk sensibly. Paula tried to read, couldn't—even though she had a brand-new Nancy Drew book—and baked butterscotch cookies to ease her mind. After the first batch was in the oven, she realized that Ahto might not be able to eat any before Peter got them all, so she made lemon pudding as well before cleaning the kitchen. Peter and about a half dozen other little boys trailed in and out, stealing cookies and leaving the TV on and clumping up and down the stairs, as if trying to squeeze as much noise as possible into the house while Ahto was away. They vanished like migrating starlings when the car drove up. Paula ran out.

"The doctor'd never heard of rachik tea, either," said Mama, "but he says it or something did him a lot of good. He wants me to bring him a sample."

"I'd like some more, please," said Ahto. "I'm cold. And could I have something to eat?"

Paula sat by him as he ate lemon pudding and drank rachik tea. "It was scary, seeing you like that," she said. "You didn't know me, and we didn't know what to do for you."

"The doctor thinks I ought to ve researched," said Ahto slowly. "He wants ne to go to the Health Science Center and ve studied." His lips were still dry and his labials more than usually slurred; but at least he could concentrate enough to finish a sentence.

"Ick," shuddered Paula. "Mama isn't going to make you, is she?"

"I don't know. I don't know if I don't want to be researched or not."

"But what if they found out you're not human?"

"Then I wouldn't have to tell lies, and when I went hone Aunt Sally and Mr. Feinan wouldn't worry about me."

This aspect of the matter had never struck Paula

before, but now she saw the force of it. When he wandered back home through the fog, she would know he was all right, but the grown-ups would be frantic. "But if they take you away from Mom, you may never get home," she said. "Wouldn't you have to go through at the same place?"

"I think so." Ahto's lids fell over his eyes as if they were too heavy to carry. "Is it true Midwinter isn't always foggy around here?"

"You can't tell what the weather'll be like, ever, except in summer it'll get hot."

"That's what Father Raven said. Maybe I should wait till after Midwinter. If I can't get back, I'll tell them, and they can take me away and study me so if I get sick again they'll know what to do." He yawned. "Or maybe I should ask Rose."

"Anyway, you don't have to decide right now." The sight of him, thin and worn out, pale on the bright sheets, made her feel soft and protective inside, as if he were a sick kitten. "You want the stereo?"

"Could you tell me a story?" he asked unexpectedly. "My mother used to tell me stories when I was sick."

So Paula told him about Bluebeard, the only story she could think of with a bird in it, and exaggerated the pigeon's role. When he fell asleep, she put Bach on the stereo and tiptoed away.

CHAPTER **15**

A Month before Midwinter

"**W**hen is Midwinter?" asked Ahto.

The grown-ups looked surprised. Tom Luther had joined them for the Thanksgiving dinner prepared by Nana and Mr. Feinman. All the leaves had been put into the dining-room table, and up till now the children had eaten resolutely while the grown-ups talked about the Christmas pageant, the warm weather, and Mr. Luther's job (he was a geologist, which as far as Ahto could tell meant a water diviner). Ahto wasn't sure if they were surprised at his speaking, or at his specific question.

"About a month," said Nana. "December twenty-first."

"The day after the Christmas pageant," clarified Mr. Feinman. "Why?"

"I think it's important."

Aunt Sally looked at him as if trying to see beneath his skin. "Is it something you remember?"

Ahto felt uncomfortable under all their eyes. He should have waited till after dinner and asked just Nana. "Sort of," he said. "Something to do with music."

"It would be," said Peter around a mouthful of marshmallowy yams. "Didn't they have anything but music on your planet?"

"Peter, how many times have I got to tell you not to tease him like that?" Aunt Sally passed the potatoes to Mr. Feinman. "You know very well he's not from another planet."

"Give Peter a break, Sal," said Mr. Luther. "How do you know he's not?"

"Tom!"

"Well, how do you, if he doesn't remember?" Mr. Luther helped himself to more ham, grinning genially. "I bet Otto'd prefer it. Why'd anybody want to be a poky old earthling? We don't have much to recommend us."

"People here are very nice," said Ahto, feeling that this was required of him as simple courtesy.

"Are they?" Mr. Luther's voice took on a sharp edge under the jolliness. "What about those bullies at school Paula told me about? What about those doctors, poking around at you?"

"The doctors want to keep me well," answered

Ahto stiffly, deliberately leaving Dan and Joe out of the discussion.

"Oh, sure. Having a brand-new condition to put their names on and write books about is irrelevant to them."

While Ahto tried to locate a reply to this puzzling remark, Aunt Sally frowned and said bitterly, "You don't need to inflict your cynicism on the kids, Tom."

"They need to learn what the world's like."

"To a large extent the world is like what you expect to find," said Mr. Feinman. "I knew a man at college . . ." and the conversation at that end of the table became grown-up again.

After dinner, Peter and Mr. Luther went into the living room to watch what seemed to be a vitally important football game. With four people clearing the table, it was done much faster than usual, but the dishes on the counter still made a small mountain. Aunt Sally started in washing vigorously, and Paula got out dishtowels, but Mr. Feinman took them away from her. "I'll dry," he said. "You and Otto go set up the Monopoly board."

Paula looked at him with a guarded expression. "Cooks don't have to do dishes," she said. "It's a rule."

"And a very good one, but I'm volunteering. Your mother and I need to talk about those Christmas pageant costumes."

Paula gave him the dishtowels and got the Monopoly game out of the hall cupboard. In the living room

Peter and Mr. Luther cheered for someone. Ahto and Nana removed the soiled cloth from the dining-room table. Dishes clattered in the kitchen. Paula unfolded the board and began counting out the money. "Amy says Mr. Feinman is sweet on Mama," she said abruptly.

"I don't see what makes Amy think it's her business to say things like that," said Nana.

"Do you think it's true?"

"I think it's not our concern."

"It will be if they get married."

Married? Ahto looked from one square, serious face to the other. The possibility had never occurred to him, but he understood about divorce by now. If Aunt Sally wasn't married to Mr. Luther anymore, then she could marry anybody she wanted to. And why not Mr. Feinman?

"Who said anything about their getting married?" asked Nana sharply.

"Nobody. But people do."

"That would be neat," said Ahto. "Then he'd live here, right?"

Paula looked at him witheringly. "Of course."

"It sure would cut down on travel time back and forth." Nana smiled. "But it doesn't look like anybody's getting married anytime soon, so you just mind your own business. Your mama can take care of herself. She's a big girl."

"I think we're fine like we are," said Paula in a flat, defiant voice.

"But you like Mr. Feinman," said Ahto, puzzled.

"I like him for my music teacher. That doesn't mean I'd like him for my daddy."

"But he wouldn't be your daddy."

Paula sighed. "You just don't understand."

"S'matter, Tom?" asked Nana, looking over their heads. "TV go out?" Which was a silly question, because they could hear Peter singing along with a Budweiser commercial. Ahto turned to see Mr. Luther, standing in the doorway between the dining and living rooms, and wondered uncomfortably whether he had heard any of the conversation. If so, he made no reaction to it.

"Where's the nearest beer?" he asked cheerfully. "Football's not football without beer."

"Then you'll have to settle for toe ball," declared Nana. "This is a dry house as long as my name's on the deed."

"There's no harm in a little beer, Flossie." Mr. Luther smiled ingratiatingly. He really did have a pleasant smile, broad and ingenuous; but it didn't soften Nana.

"We've got plenty of soda in the fridge."

"Kid stuff," snorted Mr. Luther; but he went and got a couple of Cokes, asking genially as he passed the dishwashers: "Plotting hideous deeds?"

"Just hideous costumes," answered Aunt Sally, not quite as genially. "Better put a couple more in to get cold."

Everyone tried to act as if the day were an ordinary

one, but no one was fooled. No day with Mr. Luther in it was ordinary; he made Peter fractious, Ahto uncomfortable, and put all the women, even Paula, on edge, as if he were a bottomless pit they were tiptoeing around. Mr. Feinman was too polite, Mr. Luther too jolly. Ahto wondered, if Mr. Feinman really were sweet on Aunt Sally, whether this might account for the continual exaggerations of their differences.

He could not for the life of him figure out whether Amy's rumor had any truth in it. Certainly Mr. Feinman was very nice to Aunt Sally—helping her with the dishes, changing the subject when Mr. Luther said something that visibly bothered her, selling her his GET OUT OF JAIL FREE card, which she really needed when they joined the Monopoly game, without undue haggling—but he was nice to everybody. Certainly he didn't indulge in any of the moon-eyed staring and anxious hovering that had marked Ahto's cousin's courtship of the butcher's daughter.

Mr. Luther's departure for Austin was a relief to Ahto—and, he thought, to Paula, though he wouldn't expect her to admit it. Her father's visits usually left her slightly sad and uncommunicative. Mr. Feinman stayed the rest of the day, playing gin rummy with Nana, Peter, and Aunt Sally after Paula drifted upstairs to read and Ahto conscientiously took himself off to practice his flute. He had to work extra hard at it, since it had been made for the wrong number of fingers.

Supper was an amalgamation of leftovers. As they helped themselves to pumpkin pie, Mr. Feinman turned to Ahto and asked unexpectedly: "How would you like to sing solo on Christmas Eve?"

Ahto looked at him, repeating blankly: "On Christmas Eve? Who for?"

"The candlelight service at church. Verne wants a soloist to sing 'O Holy Night' when the lights go dim and the candles are lighted, and he particularly wants you, but he was afraid you might be too shy."

"No." Ahto's mouth had suddenly dried out, though his palms were damp. "No, I wouldn't be too shy." Midwinter was four days before Christmas. What if he promised and then went home? What would everyone think of him? What if he said no, and no fog came at Midwinter? He had never sung solo. He was sure the World Bird wouldn't mind. He would like to sing solo. "Christmas is after Midwinter?" he asked, hoping the unnecessary question would signal Paula, summon forth her aid.

"They already told you that once, dummy," said Peter, burying his peach pie under a mountain of Cool Whip.

"Peter, don't you call names," said Aunt Sally sharply, "and leave some Cool Whip for other people. Four days after, Otto." She looked at him with a surprisingly knowing expression. "Do you think this important thing you almost remember about Midwinter could interfere with your singing?"

Grateful and astonished at her insight, Ahto nodded. "I think it might."

"I don't see why you shouldn't practice for it, anyway," said Paula. "You could have an understudy. All real singers and actors have understudies who can fill in for them if they get sick or something. It's in the book I'm reading."

"Now, that's so," said Mr. Feinman. "You and Steve Patterson could both practice the song. Steve's got a good enough voice to solo, but since it's breaking, that would be a reason for him to be second choice without telling him that we thought of you first. What about it, Otto? You want to try?"

"Yes, please," said Ahto promptly.

Peter was already a passive lump under a pile of covers when Ahto came to bed, to lie awake full of food and expectation. Tomorrow was a day off for everyone but Nana. They were going to go to Natural Bridge Caverns with Aunt Sally and Mr. Feinman. He remembered the cavern at home—a haunted place, where, if you stood in the entrance, you could hear the pickaxes of mountain goblins chip-chipping away at the foundations of the world. If you went too far into the pathless dark, you would most likely wander into the void at the bottom of the world and never return; or, if you did return, you would be blind and crazy. The caverns here were not like that, but well lit and, according to Aunt Sally, wonderful to look at. Of course, in San Antonio the world was round and bottomless, and mountain goblins didn't exist outside of stories. Nevertheless, the idea of the visit was pleasantly scary. It would be something to tell the children at home about, something they

144

would understand, unlike bicycles and comic books. If he ever got home.

This was the thought that kept him awake, staring at the moonlight on the wall. A month now—less—and the fog might or might not take him back. Between school, doctors, music lessons, church, friends, enemies, and all the other details of living, he sometimes went for days without thinking of home. When he did, as now, a vast loneliness opened inside him. This house was too warm, full of ugly, freakish people; composed of angles; set in the middle of a landscape as flat as a frying pan. His whole life was misty and distant, cool and unattainable beyond the glaring sun that came out even now, a mere month before Midwinter.

He wondered what his family was doing right now—if they still thought of him each day, or if, like him, they had lost the intensity of their distress in the passage of days. What would they say when they saw him again? Would his father be angry that he had gotten his tattoo alone and had sung in public? Would his mother be shocked that he had been allowed in a kitchen? Would anyone else even begin to comprehend the alien shapes and tastes and ideas that he had learned to live with?

They'll have to make all new clothes for me, he thought suddenly. Nana and Aunt Sally were letting out his clothes every three weeks, it seemed like. Would he even be recognizable as himself? His skin had weathered like a grown-up's in the fierce climate of this world.

Would he seem older than he was, or merely strange, an alien figure in his own home?

Ahto tossed and turned till the clock hands moved around nearly to eleven o'clock. He heard grown-up voices pass the stairwell, a door opening and closing. Across the hall, Paula's bed creaked. She would be spying on her mother as she said good-bye to Mr. Feinman, just as his sister used to spy on their cousin saying good-bye to the butcher's daughter. Ahto got up and padded barefoot into her room.

She was sitting up, the covers bunched around her waist, peering through the curtain. In his current mood she looked slightly monstrous, dark and hairy and lumpy—a mountain goblin in shadowy flannel. A car started, and the light cast on the curtain from the porch below went out. Paula sat back against her pillow, her face creased with discontent. "He kissed her good-night," she whispered.

"That doesn't mean anything," Ahto whispered back. "People kiss each other on TV all the time. Some of them don't even come back next episode."

"Kissing doesn't mean they'll get married," she admitted. "It means they're sweet on each other, though. She wouldn't kiss him back if she weren't sweet back." She sighed and hugged her knees.

"You wouldn't really mind too much, would you?"

"How would you like it if somebody besides your father married your mother?"

Ahto tried to imagine this, but it proved beyond his

capacity. "It couldn't happen," he said. "You can't stop being married where I come from."

"Well—but what if your father were dead?"

"She'd have to remarry, sometime. I don't guess I'd like it if she did it too soon. But men and women have to be married."

"They don't here. I'm never going to get married!"

Ahto found this whole concept too unsettling to contemplate, so he asked a question that he thought might illuminate the matter. "You'll still be able to see your father if Aunt Sally remarries—won't you?"

"Of course I will. They don't keep people from seeing their kids unless they're crazy," said Paula, in a tangle of antecedents that Ahto managed, barely, to keep straight. "But you don't care anyway. You don't even like Daddy."

The force of this accusation was considerable; Ahto fielded it as best he could. "It doesn't matter if I like him or not. With any luck I won't be around to like him next month."

Paula's face softened suddenly, as it did sometimes, into a comprehending sympathy. "Poor old Ahto! At least I get to see my daddy sometimes."

"I'm all right, mostly. Only I hope I can go home!"

"I hope so too—but I'll miss you."

"It's not fair!" exclaimed Ahto, with a sudden burst of universal bitterness. "It ought to be easier to go back and forth! What's the point of coming here and learning English and making friends and playing a five-finger flute, and then just going home and never seeing y'all again? But I don't want to stay here all the time. Why can't I just visit for a week or two?"

"Hey—in books, time runs different in different worlds. Maybe when you go back it'll still be the same Midwinter morning. Then you wouldn't be gone any time at all, and you could come back next year if you wanted."

"That doesn't make any sense. Father Raven said it had to come around to Midwinter again on both sides of the rift."

"Oh, well. I always thought that was a cop-out, anyway. I mean, it's so convenient. Nobody ever goes into a world where time goes slower than here, only faster, so they aren't missed."

"Whatshisname didn't. In the reader. The one that went to fairyland and came back three hundred years later to tell St. Patrick about it."

"Oisin. Anyway— Oh, shoot!"

Footsteps and voices mounted the stairs. Without a word, Ahto nipped across the hall to bed before Nana and Aunt Sally reached the top. When they looked in on him, he was a still, peaceful figure, the thumping of his heart invisible under the covers.

CHAPTER 16

The Christmas Pageant

Everyone, it seemed, had to do a thousand things before Christmas—presents, pageants, reports, decorations—no one had time to breathe. Ahto was almost as bewildered as he had been during his first weeks in town. What relationship could an ornamental tree in the living room, a baby in a barn, a fat man in a red suit, and winged people singing and playing harps all have with one another? Nor was it fair that his opportunity to go home should come before his opportunity to find out what was inside the mysterious packages under the tree, or that he should practice so hard for a performance he hoped he would be unable to attend.

The possibility of going home before he could sing solo at the candlelight service made the success of the school pageant that much more important. The sixth grade was doing two pieces, "Silver Bells" and "Silent Night," during which Ahto was only one of the choir. In the finale, however, he had the important part of the "partridge in a pear tree," the first of many lively presents given by "my true love." The presents were represented by children drawn from all six grades, and the rest of the school formed the choir. Ahto wondered, sometimes, where the true love expected all these maids a-milking, geese a-laying, and ladies dancing to live after Christmas was over. The rehearsals, when they went right, were a lot of fun, though.

The last day of school before Christmas break was a waste scholastically, but a great deal of fun, what with the presents and the games and the Kool-Aid. Kyle gave Paula a trick nut can out of which a spring-propelled toy monster leaped when it was opened. Nancy had drawn Ahto's name when the hat went around at school, to see who would give presents to whom. Paula had helped her pick out sheet music for him, John Denver songs—arranged for the guitar, but he did not call this to their attention. Paula had drawn a girl whom she neither knew nor cared about, while Ahto had drawn Amy. These two troublesome presents had been bought together in the mall—bath salts for one and perfume for the other. Ahto had the satisfaction of seeing Amy coerced by her own rigorous standards into thanking him politely.

The knowledge that tomorrow was Midwinter hung silent in the air as Paula, Peter, and Ahto biked home through the crisp dusk. A red VW sat in their driveway, and Paula's father on the porch. Peter sped ahead. Ahto slowed.

"You knew he was coming today," said Paula, half apologetically, half defiantly.

"Do you think he'll mind that Aunt Sally's going out to eat with Mr. Feinman after the pageant tonight?" asked Ahto.

"I don't see why." Defiance overcame apology—defiance of whom, Ahto wasn't sure. "If he didn't want her to eat out with other people, he should've stayed married to her." Paula put on a violent burst of speed and shot into the driveway, skidding sideways at the last minute in a reckless flurry of pastel skirt.

Ahto followed more sedately. "Hello, Mr. Luther," he said as Paula unlocked the door. He had been told—once—that he could call Paula's father Uncle Tom, but he didn't much want to. Not if he was going to use last names with Mr. Feinman. He went straight upstairs and stood by the window to practice his flute. No birds answered his music, though he opened the window to the gray chill on purpose. He stumbled over a simple passage; started again; stumbled; and patiently switched to scales. Do, re, mi, fa, sol, la, ti, do, do, ti, la, sol, fa, mi, re, do. Downstairs a door slammed, Peter giggled profusely, and Mr. Luther cried: "Hut!" Do, re, mi, fa, sol, la, ti, do, do, ti, la, sol, fa, mi, re, do. In less than a day it would be Midwinter. In less than five hours he would perform before the parents of the known world. Do, re, mi, fa, sol, la, ti, do. How could he possibly live that long?

Paula and Ahto made fish sticks, macaroni, and pears for dinner—possibly the last meal he would ever assist at—and they ate as soon as Nana came home. "Where's Sally?" asked Mr. Luther as they sat down. "Doesn't she get to eat?"

"She's going out on the river with Mr. Feinman after the show," said Peter. "She's his helper."

A frown flickered across Mr. Luther's face. "What on earth for?"

"Somebody's got to help him set up the stage and get all the kids into costumes," said Nana sharply.

"Why Sally?"

"Why not Sally? Not just every parent is going to have two free baby-sitters hanging around tonight."

"Daddy, what's Montezuma's revenge?" asked Paula abruptly, and a little too loudly. Everyone looked at her, and she flushed.

"What brought that on?" asked Mr. Luther.

"Carla said she was going to Mexico for Christmas vacation and Amy said she was going skiing at Vail, and Carla said Mexico was better because it was another country, but Amy said Vail was better because there was snow and you couldn't get Montezuma's revenge. But when Carla asked her what that was, she wouldn't say."

"It's—um—a real bad upset stomach," said Mr. Luther. "You get it almost any time you go to a different country, because there's always different germs in the water to what you're used to. They call it other things other places."

"What do they call it in Canada?" asked Peter.

"I don't think this is a very good subject for the dinner table," said Nana. "Ahto, aren't you going to drink your milk?"

"It's bad for my throat right before singing," said Ahto. Paula looked deep into her macaroni. Ahto wondered how long she could keep forestalling the subject of Aunt Sally and Mr. Feinman in front of her father, and if he would be around when she failed at last.

They took Nana's car, the three children in their good clothes buckling gingerly into the back, overcome with nervous giggles, Nana and Mr. Luther silent in the front. The second grade was going to sing a song about a red-nosed beast of burden, but Peter was singing a different version.

> "Randolph, the red-nosed cowboy,
> Had a very shiny gun.
> And if you ever saw it,
> You would turn around and run."

"Was he a Dallas Cowboy?" asked Ahto, just to irritate him.

"Must've been," said Paula. "I bet the sheriff's wife was a cheerleader. That's why they wanted to shoot her."

"He got tired of her saying 'Two bits, four bits, six bits, a peso—' "

"Y'all stop running down my team," Mr. Luther called back.

Ahto felt suddenly, inexplicably ill. He had an image of himself walking out in front of the known world in his partridge costume, opening his mouth, and producing no sound at all.

> "Then one foggy Saturday night,
> Sheriff came to say,
> Randolph, with your gun so bright,
> Won't you shoot my wife tonight?
> Then all the cowboys loved him—"

"That's really a disgusting song," said Paula, poking Peter in the ribs and eliciting a squeal of protest.

"I think we've heard it enough times, at that," said Nana.

"Paula poked me!"

They pulled into the parking lot. Aunt Sally was letting the Pickthorn children into the cafeteria by the side door. "Why don't y'all go backstage while we find a parking place?" suggested Nana. "And, Petie, whatever you do, don't wave at us like you did last year!"

"Don't call me Petie! That's a baby name!"

As Ahto slid out, he heard Mr. Luther ask, in a voice resembling Peter's, "Sal's not going to be backstage for the whole program, is she?" He didn't hear the answer, and he knew it anyway. Aunt Sally had promised to be there to make sure his partridge costume was ready when he had to make his quick change between "Silver Bells" and the finale. He followed the white lace bow bobbing on the back of Paula's head.

An aura of unreality clung to the whole production. Hot, milling confusion backstage—Aunt Sally and Mr. Feinman transformed into authoritative strangers—the random murmuring of waiting children overlying the songs going forward beyond the double doors. He wondered what his father would think of this proceeding and what he himself would have made of it a year ago. He closed his palms over his hand tattoos, wished he didn't have to cover up his red bird. Whatever else was different, he was himself, taller and more knowledgeable but still Ahto, destined for the priesthood; each of his songs, automatically, a sacrifice to the World Bird.

He wondered if he would throw up now or wait till he could publicly disgrace himself.

When the time came, he heard Janie speak the cue and filed on in order with the rest of the class. The audience, in the semidarkness below, was unrecognizable, and except that the room was dark and his collar scratched the back of his neck, everything went just as at rehearsal. When the lights on the risers dimmed, he stepped down sideways and slipped backstage, past the rest of the grades lining up for the finale. Aunt Sally waited with the partridge costume, keeping a watchful eye on an amalgam of costumed critters from all grades. He threw the bird mask over his head, shoved his arms into the wings, and seized the cardboard branch with its cardboard leaves and pears in plenty of time. With the first notes of "The Twelve Days of Christmas," he waddled forward as he had practiced, flourishing his branch, and sang, exactly on time and in perfect pitch, in the opening the choir made for him: "And a partridge in a pear tree!"

Not once, but twelve times, he sang it perfectly. Whatever confusion occurred among the remaining gifts—golden rings, French hens, or dancing ladies— touched him not at all. When the program was over and the groups were spotlighted for their share of applause, his was the loudest and longest.

The pageant broke up into light and chairs and families. Peter, wound up like a top; Aunt Sally and Mr. Feinman, flushed and laughing; Paula, seized with a chattering fit; Ahto, bone tired. He found himself a quiet corner where he could sit and watch everyone else cleaning up and dispersing. He wondered how much he would miss these people. They were good people. He liked them. He could fit in with them, but he could not be one of them. Even Paula, who thought of herself as an outsider, was giggling in the doorway with Nancy and Julie. Even Kyle and Roy and Renay, who were his friends, had sung ever so slightly off-key.

Because he was so tired and thoughtful, he saw the whole thing from the start—Aunt Sally and Mr. Feinman leaning on the piano; Mr. Luther walking up as if to something he owned. The cafeteria was almost empty.

"Haven't gotten to see much of you this visit, Sal," said Mr. Luther, as Nancy's mother collected her in a flurry of Spanish and left through the side door. "Why don't we go out somewhere? I'll buy you dinner."

"Sorry, Tom. Earl promised me dinner on the river, and I'm going to hold him to it."

Across the room, Rose inclined her aged head at Ahto. Even at that distance, her eyes were bright and old. Collecting Renay and two younger children, she headed out the double doors.

"I can take you to the river as well as anybody. What about it? I don't get to talk with you alone much anymore."

"There's a reason for that." Aunt Sally's voice was like the clink of ice inside a glass of tea. Nana was talking to Ms. Bingham.

"Sorry, we've already made plans." Mr. Feinman shifted his body casually, between the two of them.

Mr. Luther ignored him. "Come on, Sal. I've got to drive all the way back tonight, and I really want to talk to you about something."

"Nothing wrong with the phones in Austin, is there?" asked Aunt Sally.

He reached out. "Can't I just talk to you?"

"Not if she doesn't want you to," Mr. Feinman said.

"You mind your own business!" The tone and the expression surprised Ahto.

All the gentleness dropped out of Mr. Feinman's face. "If she doesn't want to talk to you, she doesn't have to."

"Who made you her guardian?" Mr. Luther turned and looked at Mr. Feinman as Carmen would turn and look at anybody who came near her when she had a live catch in her teeth.

"Tom," said Aunt Sally, in her warning voice; but he pressed on. The resemblance between him and Peter just now was remarkable.

"What are you hanging around her for, anyway? What business have you got letting him do it?" He turned back to Aunt Sally, his expression unchanged. "You think I don't know what's going on? You think the kids don't? Pete told me all about how late he stays! That's no way to raise my kids, Sally! If you think I'm going to put up with it, you've got another think coming!" He turned and stalked toward the door.

Mr. Feinman stood blank-faced a moment before crying out, "Now, just a minute!" and starting after him. The few remaining parents and children turned their heads to stare. Paula looked dismayed, Peter bewildered, Nana disapproving.

"Earl, forget it! It's his favorite little game—don't play it with him!"

Mr. Feinman had already almost caught up to him, not running, but making long, purposeful strides.

Ahto rose. He didn't understand what was going on, but his nerves were tight and his stomach hurt.

"Oh, God, if they have a fight I'm just going to die of embarrassment," moaned Aunt Sally.

"Don't worry." Nana patted her arm. "Tom's too chicken to fight, and Earl's got too much sense."

"There's no such thing as a man with sense," spat Aunt Sally.

Mr. Luther pushed through the door just ahead of Mr. Feinman, who followed calling, "You come back here, you—" and then there was a terrible squealing, like a ewe being slaughtered, and immediate, frozen silence.

Oddly, Ahto found that he was the first out the door. The Holubeks' car, engine running, blocked half the parking lot. The dark shape under the headlights was partly Mr. Feinman, kneeling, and partly Mr. Luther, sprawled upon the asphalt.

"I'll call nine-one-one," said Ms. Holubek briskly, her face pale in the light cast from indoors as she climbed out of the car. Her little girl wailed in the backseat, unhushed.

Ahto moved closer. No one looked at him. The world was clear and distant, like the mountains on a sunny day at home. "Better stand back till EMS gets here," said Mr. Feinman to Mr. Holubek. "It's dangerous to move an injured person."

"You can never be too careful with head wounds," said Ahto's father's voice, in his inner ear. "Especially if the victim is unconscious." The sounds of the people all around were less real to him than the words and the notes, his father's voice rising and falling, indescribably pure.

Mr. Feinman looked up as Ahto knelt beside him— not at Ahto, but beyond. Of the two faces, Mr. Feinman's was the more stricken. Mr. Luther looked peaceful to Ahto, just as Hahz had, a year ago, when he'd fallen and hit his head on the rocky hillside. "I'm sorry, Sally," said Mr. Feinman. "It's my fault. He looked back when I called and tripped on the curb and fell right in front of the car. They stopped in time, but he hit his head on the fender. I'm sorry."

"It's not your fault," said Aunt Sally, somewhere above and behind Ahto. "Shouldn't we cover him?"

Feeling the right notes forming solid in the back of his throat, Ahto began to sing. He did not touch Mr. Luther or listen anymore to what was going on around him, and when Mr. Feinman tried to take him away, he fought against him, because you can't take chances with head wounds, and, wherever he was, he was the servant of the World Bird, entrusted with the healing music. He thought it was Paula and Nana who got them to leave him alone.

At last the ambulance arrived, and when the competent, uniformed people descended upon the still form, Ahto fell silent. He was very cold. He couldn't tell anything about the color of the face under the headlights, but Mr. Luther groaned when he was touched. Mr. Feinman and the Holubeks were talking with a policeman. Paula called, her eyes huge and still in her face. "Ahto! Ahto, come on! You'll catch your death!"

He followed her indoors, shivering and tired. "You were fixing him, weren't you?" Paula asked in a low voice.

"I was trying." Ahto blinked, his eyes watery with weariness and the glare of electric light. Nana bore them away to the car. Aunt Sally joined them in a moment. "The EMS people say it doesn't look bad, considering," she said, with false, bright cheeriness.

"There's no point in our following them to the hospital. He's going to be all right."

The ambulance passed, red lights rotating and flashing, as she started the car. Ahto wondered what had happened to her dinner with Mr. Feinman, but didn't like to ask. Peter, his face grubby and damp, fell asleep slumped against the car door, and Nana had to carry him up to bed. It was nearly eleven, and nobody mentioned baths, so Ahto got straight into his pajamas and brushed his teeth. On the way out of the bathroom he ran into Paula.

"Tomorrow's Midwinter," he said, sounding flat to himself.

"I know," said Paula miserably.

Next morning the alarm under Ahto's pillow went off at four. He rolled over, snuggled deeply into the covers, and then remembered why he had set it so early. Wrapped in his robe, he tiptoed to the window and opened the curtains. Beyond, darkness stretched across the world, unsoftened by the paleness of fog.

Two hours later, he still sat by the window, and dawn was rising clearly across the sky.

CHAPTER 17

The Night before Christmas

"**S**o are you going to tell them or aren't you?" asked Paula.

"I will," said Ahto. "Everything's all complicated right now."

"They won't believe you anyway," declared Peter. "They'll put you in the funny farm. I wish you'd told them last week, so you'd be at the funny farm and we could have turkey tomorrow."

They were playing Pick-Up-Stix on the dining-room table. In the living room, the Christmas tree winked hypnotically above piles of bright packages, Carmen stretched herself along the couch, and the stereo played carols. Rain fell with dull determination. Underneath the superficial noises, Ahto could feel the silence. Nana was upstairs with a book. Aunt Sally was visiting Mr. Luther at the hospital. It was Christmas Eve.

"Daddy's doing fine 'cause of you," said Paula. "I bet if you hadn't helped him, he would've died or been brain damaged or something. Peter, stop jiggling the table."

"I'm not."

Ahto waited for the surface quiver to cease and eased a green stick off a yellow one. "I'd rather tell everybody all at once. To get it over with." Almost free, the green stick rolled, slid, and fell, creating a new pattern. "Cripes."

"You mean Mama and Nana and Mr. Feinman?"

"Uh-huh. And Mr. Feinman hasn't come over since the pageant."

Peter knelt up in his chair, leaning over the table and squinting at the tangle of sticks. "That's 'cause he knows it's his fault Daddy got run over," he announced, passing over two sure targets for a deceptively simple heap.

"That's not true," said Paula sharply. "Daddy ran out in the street his own self. Nobody pushed him."

"But Mr. Feinman was chasing him. Mama said it was my fault when I chased Carmen on top of the vanity and knocked Nana's makeup around."

"Daddy's got more sense than a cat. You moved that yellow one."

"Did not."

"Did too."

"Did not."

"There! You moved it that time, anyway."

Peter sat down again. Paula picked up two sticks in rapid succession.

"It is too Mr. Feinman's fault," said Peter sullenly.

"Just shut up."

"Why are you always on his side? It's Mr. Feinman's fault and he knows it and that's why he don't come over anymore."

"I'm not on his side. I'm just fair. If Daddy'd looked where he was going, he wouldn't've run out in front of the car. Right, Ahto?"

Ahto opened his mouth to answer, but Peter flung his voice across both of them.

"Ahto doesn't count. He's always on Mr. Feinman's side!"

"And you're always on Daddy's!"

"Somebody has to be!" Peter's shout was half a wail. "Nana doesn't like him, and Mama hardly likes him at all anymore, and Ahto only likes people who like him first, and now you act like you don't like him anymore either!"

Paula stopped with the stick she was working on half out of the pile and stared at him.

"He's my daddy and I like him and I'll always be on his side!" Peter howled. "Always, always, always! And they won't let me in the hospital to see him and it's not fair!"

Ahto sat uneasy in the long, cold moment hanging between their two faces. It seemed forever before Peter leaped up, shaking the table so that all the sticks rolled free, and thundered out of the room. Carmen jumped, alert at his passage.

Ahto felt he ought to say something. "He doesn't understand anything, really. He's too little."

"I do like Daddy," said Paula miserably. "Only—it was his own fault he got run over. I can see that and still like him, can't I?" Paula scooped up the Pick-Up-Stix and packed them away.

"You want to call Nancy or Kyle or somebody and see if they're doing anything?"

"Naw." Paula pushed her chair back, still looking unhappy. "I think I'll go read."

Peter had turned up the TV and was staring at a cartoon upon which he had often and relentlessly piled scorn. Paula trailed upstairs. Ahto followed, and tried to practice his flute.

Aunt Sally returned late because she had stopped at the grocery store. Ahto helped her put things away and then lay out ingredients for special, last-minute baking. "Where is everybody?" she asked. Peter was still staring at the television and had not turned to look at her since she'd come in.

"I think Nana fell asleep," answered Ahto. "Peter and Paula had a fight."

Aunt Sally sighed. "Those two are going to get coal in their stockings."

"Aunt Sally, are you mad at Mr. Feinman?"

Her hands still in the refrigerator, she turned her

head to pass him a surprised look. "No. Should I be?"

"Peter's mad at him. He says it's Mr. Feinman's fault about the accident."

"Oh, that's silly." Aunt Sally pushed the door closed with her foot and looked thoughtful. "But you show me a man who isn't silly, and I'll show you a woman in disguise." Before Ahto could protest this slander on his sex, she continued. "Mr. Feinman doesn't think I'm mad at him, does he?"

"I don't know. He doesn't act normal anymore."

"As if I didn't have enough troubles! Ahto, when you see Mr. Feinman tonight before the candlelight service, you tell him I'm expecting him for eggnog afterward. Tell him Mr. Luther's fine and will be getting out tomorrow."

Ahto blinked at her. "Tomorrow!"

Aunt Sally smiled. "Yes, tomorrow. For Christmas. You want to go tell my feuding children what they missed hearing because they were too busy sulking to be nice to their mother?"

Ahto pounced on Peter first, then ran upstairs feeling better than he had since the pageant. Everyone would cheer up with this news. He would have all three important grown-ups here tonight and could unburden himself of the lies he had been carrying. He didn't even mind that Mr. Luther would be in the house, probably all day, tomorrow. You couldn't feel really hostile to a man you had sung healing songs over for half an hour.

When Mr. Feinman came to pick him up early for the candlelight service, Ahto ran out in a highly nervous state, the tattoo in each palm damp. "All ready to sing solo?" asked Mr. Feinman.

"I guess so. My mouth is all dry."

"That'll pass. I'm glad whatever was supposed to happen at Midwinter didn't come off. Steve's mother called me a while ago and said not to pick him up—he has a cold in his throat. We'd've been up the creek without a soloist if you hadn't been able to make it."

Mr. Feinman had been careful, all this time, not to press him on the subject of Midwinter, but he was visibly curious nonetheless. Ahto was glad he'd be able to explain tonight. "Aunt Sally said she'd expect you for eggnog after services," he said.

"Did she?" Mr. Feinman's voice had an odd note. The rain had stopped. A shadowy world of reflection and unreality passed outside the car. "That's nice of her."

"Not particularly," said Ahto. That didn't sound right, so he added, "I think she misses you coming over. She has to go to work every day and then go see Mr. Luther and she gets tired." He found lurking in his vocabulary a grown-up phrase that seemed useful in this case. "She doesn't have enough friends her own age."

Mr. Feinman looked at him and shook his head. "Why are you so much older than other kids?"

It had been a long time since Ahto had doubted his comprehension of English, but this sentence made no sense as he heard it. He blinked against the headlights of an oncoming car. "Sir?"

"Never mind. How's her—how's Mr. Luther?"

Ahto grinned at him. "Getting out tomorrow."

"Great!" Yes, he was plainly relieved. "I suppose he'll be visiting tomorrow."

"Mm-hmm."

"You don't look very enthusiastic."

"Um . . . I mean . . ." He floundered and found a harmless generality. "I was just thinking, it was a shame everybody couldn't be happy at Christmas."

"Yes, it is." Mr. Feinman was smiling, looking more like himself than usual. "Be nice if everybody's feelings fitted neatly into everybody else's, wouldn't it?"

"Uh—yes," said Ahto, taking the easy way out of the conversation. Mr. Feinman laughed for no apparent reason. Ahto relaxed.

They pulled into the church parking lot as the rain started again—a fine mist, smelling cold and fresh. They hurried in and soon all awkward feelings and desires were tidied away under the requirements of the music. Ahto found that his nervousness had fled, and only one thing still troubled him. "I wish my father could be here," he whispered to Mr. Feinman as they waited to file into the choir stall. Mr. Feinman patted his back. The organist started to play "O Come All Ye Faithful."

Ahto had gotten used to the way Methodists did things and found he could listen with comfortable enjoyment to the story of God being born as a child in a stable, though during the prayer he still addressed his supplications to the World Bird. The minister said Christmas was a time of rejoicing, so he thought of all the things he had to rejoice over in his exile and found a surprising lot of them. When he did get home, he would know more about more things than any other boy of his tattoo year, would know more about some things than the priests; and he would have brand-new kinds of music to offer to the World Bird.

When the lights dimmed and the flame passed from candle to candle along the pews of well-dressed, familiar people, Ahto felt that the clear, sweet voice rising from his throat to fill the sanctuary was not his doing, but a gift from something outside—Jesus or the World Bird, it made no never mind—and that he could admire the effect without vanity.

At home afterward, the eggnog was cold and sweet. The grown-ups talked about Mr. Luther, and the service, and grown-up sorts of things. Peter went upstairs, protesting, to his bath. The Christmas tree winked at itself in the dark window. Paula picked up one of the packages with her name on it and shook it. Ahto sat beside her, absently shaking one of his own.

"That's clothes," said Paula confidently. "You can tell by the way everything slides in a soft-sounding lump." She frowned thoughtfully at the ones in her hands. "I think Nana must've disguised this one on purpose. It doesn't rattle at all."

"I don't know how to start off telling them," said Ahto. "Cripes, I've been lying to them most of the year!"

"That's true. But that was my fault. I told you to."

"I didn't have to do what you said."

"Tell you what—I'll tell them that part."

"What are you two whispering about?" asked Nana. "Figuring out what Santa's going to bring?"

"No," said Paula. "Nana, if I talked Ahto into telling a lie when he was still getting used to things and didn't understand English too good, it'd be my fault, not his, right? Because I was the one explaining things to him and he couldn't help it if I explained wrong."

Nana looked taken aback and sidestepped the question. "Has he been telling lies?"

"Only because I told him to!"

"I knew better," Ahto said hastily, not liking the role of dupe she was thrusting upon him. "Only I didn't want to go to the funny farm."

"What are you kids talking about?" asked Mr. Feinman.

Ahto looked at the three grown-ups ranged around, observing him with interest, and took a deep breath as if he were going to sing. "I never had amnesia."

"He's from another world," said Paula helpfully. "Like Narnia or something."

The grown-ups exchanged glances. Nana reached down from the couch and picked Carmen up, who rubbed faces with her and settled down to purr. Ahto couldn't tell if they believed Paula or not.

"It's true," he said defensively. "Father Raven explained it to me."

"And you know the doctors and science teachers are always saying how strange he is," supplied Paula. "I mean, there's never been anybody with just three fingers before! And that's because Ahto's not human." She faltered. "You won't lock him up, will you? He's not crazy. I saw him come. Peter did, too. That's why he's always going on about space aliens."

"No one will lock you up, Otto," said Aunt Sally kindly, adding, with some hesitation, "not if I can help it. Why don't you tell us the whole truth now, and we'll see what's best to do."

So Ahto told them, Paula sitting quiet chewing her lip and occasionally bursting out irrepressibly with a reference to some book. The grown-ups seemed particularly interested in hearing about the valley at home, and what he had learned there about healing, and music, and life in general. When he told them about being born to the priesthood, Mr. Feinman nodded. "That's what you were doing the night Paula's father got run over, wasn't it? One of your father's healing songs?"

"Yes," said Ahto. "It's part of my job." Certainly they were taking the matter seriously, but he couldn't help reflecting that they'd be equally serious if they thought he were crazy. Nana did not look comfortable, despite the cat in her lap.

"It's all rather hard to swallow," said Aunt Sally. "Except that, here you are, and your being from somewhere else makes all the odd things about you perfectly natural."

"It's scientific," said Paula triumphantly. "Like Mr. Rodriguez says—the somethinged razor—it's the simplest idea that covers all the facts."

"I wouldn't go so far as to say it satisfies Occam's razor," said Aunt Sally in her best austere, grown-up voice.

"I don't know, though," said Mr. Feinman. "Sometimes when I think about how he must have been raised before he came to us, to have turned out like this—it seems to me to be simpler to believe he came out of a spaceship or an interdimensional warp."

Peter thundered on the stairs. "You're just going to have to let us think on this awhile," said Nana briskly. "Meanwhile it's bathtime. Don't forget to brush your teeth."

Ahto went upstairs feeling vaguely let down. If that was all that was going to happen, he could have told them ages ago. He was rather subdued through the rest of the evening, even when they closed the day with a ritual—reading a poem called "The Night Before Christmas" and singing "Silent Night." As they went upstairs, however, Paula added a more satisfactory note.

"They don't want to talk about it in front of us," she said, "but I overheard them in the kitchen. They're going to sound out one of the doctors who said you barely seemed human, and see what he thinks."

"One of them said that? Why didn't anybody tell me?"

"Grown-ups won't tell you things like that if they can help it. Mama'll talk to him after New Year's. There's no point doing anything before then."

"Why not?" asked Ahto.

"You still don't know anything, do you?" Paula laughed.

Next day Mr. Luther and Mr. Feinman both visited. Mr. Luther was pale and cheerful. They were polite to each other, and the air was more relaxed than it had ever been before with Mr. Luther in the house. Once, they were in the kitchen at the same time, and Ahto walked in on the tail end of a conversation.

"—never got over being jealous of Sally," Mr. Luther was saying, from the depths of the refrigerator.

"I can't blame you for that," said Mr. Feinman, slicing pie. "But she doesn't seem to be the kind who's flattered by it."

"This is true." Mr. Luther turned—carefully, for he was still occasionally unsteady in his head—and saw Ahto. His smile looked perfectly genuine, and he met Ahto's eyes for the first time. "Hi, sport. Which pie you after?"

"Pumpkin, please," said Ahto, startled. Something had changed somewhere, and he didn't have to understand what to feel that the complicated web of people—Aunt Sally and Mr. Feinman, Mr. Feinman and Mr. Luther, Mr. Luther and himself, on and on, around—was sorting itself out. He and Paula would not have to tangle with it anymore.

CHAPTER **18**

The Rift in the Fog

Paula had wakened to the sound of soft music a quarter of an hour ago, but she was still curled tight under the covers, staring blind out the window. The universe ended a few feet from her pane, vanishing in a roil of white fog. The glass breathed coolness into her warm face, putting an edge on her intense comfort.

Daddy had gone home to Austin under his own power, wearing the shirt she had given him. Mr. Feinman had taken Mama out on a real date, with dinner and dancing and getting home late, and even Peter had not minded. Mama was talking about adopting Ahto. That could get complicated, but—

Cripes, she thought idly. Why couldn't this fog happen when it was supposed to? She yawned and

174

rolled over to punch her snooze alarm. At a distance of five inches, the red digits resolved into 4:30. The music did not stop.

A raven croaked.

Paula sat up. The music was faint beyond the fog, like a choir three blocks away. Fog, white and featureless, just like the day she had met Ahto—the day school started last year—two days after New Year's—

"Oh!" exclaimed Paula, seizing her glasses and jumping into the sudden chill of the room. "Oh, we are so dumb!"

She met Ahto at the door to the boys' room, fully dressed in jeans, tennis shoes, and the red poncho, now too short, over a long-sleeved shirt. "Ahto!" she whispered, remembering Mama and Nana slumbering near. "Ahto, Midwinter in your world doesn't match up to Midwinter here! It matches up to two days after New Year's!"

"Father Raven just explained it to me," Ahto whispered back exultantly. "I'm going home!"

"Wait up, will you?" grumbled Peter in the background. "I want to go, too."

"I've got to write Nana and Aunt Sally a note." The eager glow in Ahto's face was suddenly acutely painful. "If you hurry and get dressed, you can come see me off."

Paula, feeling empty and sore inside, pulled jeans and a sweater on over her pajamas. Of course she was glad he was going home, where nobody would stare at his nose and tattoos and fingers, where he would be normal and could do things that seemed normal to him. Of course she was.

Only, who would she talk to about important things—books and music and other worlds? What would happen to the group of boys and girls who hung out together as friends because Ahto's abnormality formed a bridge between the sexes? Would Mr. Feinman still like Mama without Ahto around? What would it hurt, if Otto stayed an extra year? Hardly anybody made fun of him anymore.

Swallowing her discomfort, Paula tiptoed downstairs. Ahto was going back where he belonged, and it was a good thing, and she was glad for him. Everything else would keep till he was gone.

Ahto had just propped a note against the toaster when she came downstairs. The back door stood open, letting cold air in. "Peter's getting the bikes out," he whispered, though the electric light made whispering sound funny. "You know, this is probably the last time I'll ever be in a kitchen."

"Maybe you'll change the taboos and get liberated," suggested Paula.

Ahto shook his head. "There's too much work to do. If we didn't divide it up, it'd never get done. I'll miss baking cookies, though."

They turned the light off and shut the door behind them as they went into the ghostly morning. "Aren't you even going to take your flute?" asked Peter, rolling impatiently back and forth on his bike.

"It's Mr. Feinman's flute," said Ahto, mounting. "Ready?"

The music was louder, directionless in a world without landscape. Father Raven fluttered out of nowhere, ruffled and cross looking, to perch on Ahto's handlebars. Their bicycle lights made yellow patches on the white fog without noticeably improving the visibility. The children rode slowly, single file, glancing around for anything to hook their eyes on, and finding nothing. Ahto began to sing along with the music, softly.

"Kark!" exclaimed Father Raven, flapping awkwardly into the air. Ahto pulled up, his front wheel on dead grass. The slap of water lay faint beneath the singing. Even the lighthouse was invisible. Peter jigged up and down to keep warm.

"This is worse than the day we found you," he said. "Where's your spaceship?"

"There isn't one," said Ahto patiently. "I've told you, all I do is walk. That way."

Paula followed the direction of his finger into featureless white. She could feel her own heart, a disturbing sensation. Unfamiliar though it was, the music was beautiful, a path of sound marking the way through oblivion. How often had she longed to walk out of this world and into another, like a person in a book? Here it was, her big chance, there just for her to take—

"What if I come with you?" she asked abruptly.

"If you go I go too!" shouted Peter immediately.

Just what she needed to spoil everything! "Don't be dumb. You'd have to stay and tell Mama where I went."

"That's not fair! I want to go too!"

"What if there's no fog here next year?" asked Ahto.

"Then there would be the year after that," said Paula recklessly.

"You're not going without me!" protested Peter.

"It would be nice to show you things," said Ahto thoughtfully.

Father Raven circled low over their heads. "Kark!" he said impatiently.

Ahto glanced up at him and nodded. "I've got to go now. Are you coming or not?"

As Paula hesitated, a rift opened in the fog. She couldn't see into it, precisely; but a light streamed through and the music swelled. Ahto stood at the edge of it, his flat, naked face flushed almost pink, waiting. Peter bumped against her side, took a step toward the light. He looked small and cold, his pajamas sticking out around his edges. The sight decided her. Before she could change her mind, Paula took hold of the edge of his jacket. "It wouldn't be nice to Mama and Nana," she said firmly. "Good-bye, Ahto. Have a good life."

"I'll send you a message next year, if I can," said Ahto. "Good-bye." He turned and strode, singing, into the fog and the light, the mist rising to obscure his ankles, the raven flying above and just ahead.

Cold and heavy inside, Paula watched him go. Peter stamped from foot to foot, surprisingly silent. Ahto's familiar, sweet voice blended in with the others', as incomprehensible as Mr. Feinman's Bach albums. There goes the magic, walking out of my life, thought Paula. The fine sound of the phrase made her feel better. She began to hum the tune, which must be the Midwinter hymn Ahto had told her about. Ahto's figure grew dim, the mist closing behind him as he walked farther and farther out across the invisible lake. Far away, a raven croaked. The light and music faded. The mist closed into a wall again.

Peter sneezed. "I wish we could've gone too."

"Well, we couldn't," said Paula crossly, already regretting her decision. She could feel the tears burning behind her face, but she couldn't give in to them in front of Peter. "Let's go home before we catch our deaths."

"What about Ahto's bike?" asked Peter.

"Leave it. I'll come and get it as soon as the fog thins out."

Paula pedaled slowly, not looking behind her, keeping an eye out for cars and other fog-shrouded dangers. Peter rode rings around her, raucously trying to sing the tune that had come from the fog. "Kyle and Roy and everybody's going to be mad they didn't see him go," he interrupted himself.

"They'll just have to be mad, then." Paula wondered about Renay's grandmother. A year in Otherwhere hadn't hurt her any. Maybe she should've gone. Maybe—

The lights of home glowed through the fog as they rode up, and Mama was just coming out, wrapped in her housecoat. When she saw them, her cross, worried look changed to cross relief. "Where've y'all been?" she demanded. "And where's Otto?"

Peter dropped his bike in the yard and ran to her. "Ahto went home, Mama! The raven came and got him and he went straight out over the lake and this choir was singing and Paula wouldn't let me go!"

A change came over those familiar, square features. "Gone? He—just went away?"

"He left a note." Paula parked her bike decently on the sidewalk. She had never seen her mother look like that before, not even when Daddy got run over. "The calendars don't match up properly. Midwinter there is two days after New Year's here and it was foggy both places and—"

"Gone," said Mama.

Suddenly, Paula was glad she hadn't followed Ahto. She ran up the steps, threw her arms around her mother's waist, and said into a faceful of terry cloth: "He'll send a message next time it's foggy two days after New Year's."

"Will he?" choked Mama.

They went inside to break the news to Nana.

The music was better than any landmark. When the fog closed behind him, when the lighthouse loomed on his right, Ahto quickened his pace. Father Raven circled back.

"Come along, come along! Once the music stops, there's no telling where you'll turn up!"

Ahto started running, ceasing his singing to save his breath. The surface under his sneakers changed, became hard and slanted. He had walked on flat surfaces for so long he stumbled and almost fell into the fog before his feet remembered how to compensate. The music swelled, three-quarters of the way through the hymn. This year's crop of boys would be at the animal pens by now, driving their charges in.

He nearly ran into the rock before he saw it. Father Raven lighted atop it, where the mountain cat had crouched so long ago, and smoothed his wings. "You can find your way home from here without me, I reckon."

"Yes, sir," panted Ahto, leaning his pattering heart against the cold stone. He was really home now, touching his own world with his own hands! "Thank you, Father Raven!"

"Prrp! Came that close to missing you! I'd clean forgot about the difference in cycles. Getting old, that's what I am."

"Father Raven, come with me. You can stay in my aviary."

"Not me, boy! Lot of messy, noisy birds—no, thanks!" He paused in preening to cock an eye at Ahto. "Reckon I'll stop by, see how you're doing, once in a while. See you around." With a rattle of feathers, he launched himself again, toward the upland pastures.

The hymn was approaching its finale. Ahto followed the path downward, adding the alien prints of sneakers to the fresh marks of sandals and hooves. The air stank cozily of damp wool. The singing died, leaving him alone with looming shadows, echoing bleats, and, ahead, the chuckle of the brook tumbling over rocks on its way down the valley.

First the flocks began to bawl; then he saw, clear and solid out of the fog, the pyramidal home of the butcher. The soft village road lay under his feet. He began to run, past hogans that looked like hogans, into the village center—into the crowd of properly dressed, properly designed people—just as the first boy emerged from the tattooing shed. Startled, noseless faces turned toward him; musical voices gasped and murmured, and his father stopped in the act of taking the second boy by the hand. For a moment the world paused; then the babble broke out all around, a gust of wind blew the fog aside, familiar arms caught him up, and he was home.

PENI R. GRIFFIN was born in Harlington, Texas, but moved around a lot before finally settling in San Antonio with her husband. She has had several short stories published in science fiction and fantasy magazines. She has recently written her second book for young readers, *A Dig in Time*.

An out-of-this-world adventure!

Journey to Terezor

by Frank Asch

Matt and his parents are about to be washed away by a flood when they are miraculously saved and transported to a strange new planet. After a while, Matt doesn't think that life on S-15 is too bad, but his friends Ryan and Sara are sick of being treated like interstellar zoo specimens. The two begin to plan a daring break for freedom—and before he knows it, Matt's caught up in it too. While Ryan and Sara face permanent molecular restructuring as punishment for their treason, Matt must flee to another colony of endangered aliens, and barely escapes with his life. But the worst part is when they find themselves face-to-face with the last terrifying Terezor in existence!

"Fast-action adventures…a quick, exciting trip to other worlds." —*Booklist*

A BULLSEYE BOOK PUBLISHED BY ALFRED A. KNOPF, INC.

Little by little, they were drawn...

Into the Dream

by William Sleator

Every night it's the same dream—the strange one about the field, the big glowing thing, and the eerie figure in white. At first, Paul thinks it's just a recurring nightmare. But then he finds out that Francine, a girl in his class, is having it too. Realizing that it must mean something, Paul and Francine join forces and soon learn that the dream is really a child's desperate cry for help. Feeling the urgency, the two delve deeper and deeper into the dream. Can they find the mystery boy before their dream becomes terrifying reality?

"A thriller of top-notch quality." —*Booklist*

"A compelling fantasy written with increasing tempo and suspense."
　　　　　—*The Bulletin of the Center for Children's Books*

A BULLSEYE BOOK PUBLISHED BY ALFRED A. KNOPF, INC.